57

TARGET WESTMINSTER

TARGET
WESTMINSTER

B. M. Gill

Hodder & Stoughton

First published in Great Britain in 1977
by Robert Hale Limited

First paperback edition published in 1994
by Hodder and Stoughton
Simultaneous hardback edition published in 1995
by Hodder and Stoughton
A division of Hodder Headline PLC

British Library Cataloguing in Publication Data

Gill, B. M.
Target Westminster
I. Title
823.914 [F]

ISBN 0 340 62552 X

Typeset by CBS, Felixstowe, Suffolk

Printed and bound in Great Britain by
Mackays of Chatham, Chatham, Kent

Hodder and Stoughton Ltd
A division of Hodder Headline PLC
338 Euston Road, London NW1 3BH

Target Westminster

ONE

It was a coincidence, David told himself, it wasn't contrived. His wife's startled expression as she watched Mackilroy and the girl crossing the restaurant floor towards them wasn't lost to him. The first sharp stab of shock and anger gave way to relief. This wasn't Dee's doing. Their fifth wedding anniversary celebration which was also Dee's twenty-fifth birthday wasn't being deliberately sabotaged. She hadn't known that Mackilroy was coming. Mackilroy couldn't have known that they would be here. He had decided on the Silver Swan restaurant less than a week ago and his secretary at the ministry had booked the table. It was absurd to believe that after three years of – he honestly believed – non-communication between Dee and Mackilroy that Mackilroy could have a sixth sense that led him here now. Even if he had, why trail another girl along with him?

His parliamentary training had taught him to put the right face on to suit the occasion and when he stood up he was smiling.

'Hello, Mack. Back in London again?' It was trite. Stupid. Obvious. But at least his voice sounded normal. Friendly, even.

Mackilroy's dark eyes were on Dee. She felt the glance physically with a gut response that she had believed decently dead. It was like seeing the re-play of an old film that was resurrected from the archives and was momentarily more real than the present. She and Mack had met in a hotel in Aberdeen. He had been doing some freelance reporting on the oil industry and its effect on the local people. She and David – two years married – had been on a touring holiday of the area. Due to a combination of circumstances that she sometimes thought of as fate – the car had broken down and needed a major repair at the precise moment that David had been urgently recalled to settle some trouble in the constituency – she had stayed on in Aberdeen to await the car and David had returned to London by train. What followed – if not inevitable – had been irresistible. She deplored it. She regretted it. Until now she had almost forgotten it – almost but not quite . . .

Mackilroy said, 'Yes. I flew in from Belfast last week.' The slight burr in his voice showed both Irish and Scottish ancestry.

The girl behind him made a small impatient movement reminding him that she was there. He drew her forward. 'Briony Prantella. Dee and David Berringer. May we bring our drinks over and join you?'

David said, 'Why not?' because he couldn't say anything different. The anniversary celebration was capable of standing a twosome intrusion. Mackilroy on his own would have been harder to take. He tried to play host with some semblance of enthusiasm. 'Had you come earlier you could have joined us in a meal. Have you dined?'

The girl answered for the two of them. 'We've eaten.'

Mackilroy observed, 'A subtle distinction. We had a grill in Charley's Coffee House.' He went over to the bar through the archway at the far end of the room and came back with a whisky for himself and a shandy for Briony. He had noticed that David and Dee were having brandy with their coffee. 'Shall I freshen yours up?'

'Not just yet, thanks.' David looked at Dee. She hadn't spoken a word. Her face was calm, but the tension showed in her hands.

Mackilroy raised his glass to her before sitting next to Briony. 'Happy birthday, Dee.'

'You remembered?' She was surprised, pleased.

'Of course.' He had also remembered that it was her wedding

2

anniversary, but had no intention of commenting on it. She was wearing a gold and emerald bracelet. Berringer's anniversary present, probably.

Dee followed his glance and guessed what he was thinking. Yes, it was a beautiful present. Yes, the marriage had survived. She wondered if the oddly-named girl-friend was going through the same maelstrom of emotions with Mack that she had gone through with him. She made herself smile at the girl.

'Did you fly over with Mack?'

'No. I was here first.' It was abrupt.

'You're a journalist, too?'

'No.' The idea suddenly struck her as funny. 'God, no!' When she laughed she looked about nineteen. She wore a scarlet tank top over brown slacks. Her arms were thin and bony and scattered with freckles. Her laughter was nervous rather than amused.

'You have a job?'

'I work – yes.'

Dee was asking questions for the sake of her own equanimity. She didn't care what the girl did. If she didn't want to tell her then that was her affair. The main thing was to talk – about something – about anything.

'Do you work, Mrs Berringer?'

The question was being sharply patted back.

'I was David's secretary until we married.'

'But you don't work now?'

'My dear Briony,' Mackilroy chided, 'the wives of important parliamentarians open bazaars and receive bouquets and smile – smile – smile. Dee hasn't sullied her fingers with anything so mundane as a typewriter or word processor since David began trailing clouds of glory.'

David, determined not to be needled, smiled blandly. Dee was beginning to look ruffled and slightly annoyed. He waited for her to explain about her work in the constituency.

3

Mack stopped her just as she started. 'I know. I shouldn't tease you.' He hadn't intended to make her cross. An argument was the last thing he wanted. His Celtic impetuosity tended to make him less than tactful. Berringer, he thought, was keeping his cool remarkably well. In retrospect, he always had – choosing to ignore rather than challenge. The affair – never overt – had been held in check by Berringer's tactical handling of it. For him – on the surface, at least – it hadn't been sufficiently serious for comment. Fires not stoked tended to die out. If he had flared up into accusation this meeting wouldn't be taking place here now. He was ten years older than Dee and at thirty-five probably one of the youngest Defence Ministers the country had known. Mack had accused Dee of remaining with him because he had a lot to offer her materially. The accusation, angrily refuted by her, had been made as a sop to his own pride. She had remained for some reason best known to herself, but it wasn't avarice. And it couldn't have been pity, either. Berringer was too strong to inspire it. Then why? He looked at them covertly. Dee, dark hair piled high accentuating the upward sweep of her eyebrows, was in profile to him as she gave her husband a sudden small rueful smile. He was looking back at her amused. Some shared joke about her constituency work – perhaps. Yes, the marriage was surviving and by the look of it very well.

The assumption was correct, then.

But naturally. Nothing had been left to chance.

They began talking about Northern Ireland.

Briony who had been listening but not contributing got up abruptly. 'I need the loo.' She made her way past the tables and then out through the bar.

Dee half rose. 'That's the wrong way.'

Mack said, 'Leave her. She'll find it.'

'The conversation wasn't upsetting her, was it? Is she Irish?'

'No, it wasn't upsetting her. But it isn't the most cheerful of subjects.'

4

David agreed. Holidays seemed an innocuous topic. The Scottish holiday – like a scorpion on a rock – was carefully skirted around. No one mentioned it. Dee and David had been cruising the Greek Islands during the summer recess. David mimicked the Greek courier with considerable skill and had them laughing. All tension was dissipated.

Mack steered the conversation the way he wanted it steered. 'The best way of getting around is by adapting a van. I bought one a couple of years ago and did it up – bunk – flap-down table – bottled gas for cooking. It's parked outside now. Like to come and see it?'

Dee asked, 'What – now?' There was disappointment in her voice. To get up and go meant an end of the evening.

David, glad of a civilized and early ending, showed no reluctance. 'If you'll just wait until I settle the bill . . .' He stood up and looked around for the waiter.

Mack pointed out that by the time he caught his eye Briony would be back. 'The van is parked by the front entrance. We'll wait for the two of you there.' He picked up Dee's wrap and gave it to her.

Dee looked at David and he shrugged. Obviously he couldn't leave without paying the bill, but Briony was Mack's responsibility and he resented having to wait for her. It seemed churlish to make a fuss. He hoped she wouldn't be long.

The night air was sharp and Dee shivered as she felt it on her bare arms. She drew her wrap around her and followed Mack down the entrance steps and towards the van. She knew now that it was a deliberate ploy to give them a few moments on their own together. She hoped he wouldn't ask her about her marriage – about David. The storm of loving Mack and then breaking off the relationship had been as violently traumatic as a landscape razed by a hurricane. She hoped he wouldn't touch her now. She hoped he would. The London air was thick with diesel fumes and the constant roar of passing cars held her to the present. The past was finished and dead and done with.

The van, mud-spattered and painted grey, was parked near the exit gate. He opened the passenger door. 'Let me help you up. It's higher than a normal car.'

His hand was on her wrist and his arm around the small of her back. The contact was brief – too brief. They had first slept together in the hotel in Aberdeen. She had felt a traitor to David on the following day and had been miserably self-accusing. The following day. There was always a following day. But there was also a now.

He got into the driving seat beside her.

'Dee,' There was an urgency in his voice – almost a peremptoriness. 'Dee – look at me.'

She couldn't see his face clearly in the darkness of the van. 'Yes – what is it?' Disturbed by something in his attitude that she didn't understand she threw up a fence of words to hold him away from her. 'You wanted to show me the van. Well, I'm here. Show me. Your conversion. What you've done. We can't see anything just sitting here. Are there doors at the back? . . . Mack, what's the matter?'

'I said – look at me.'

'Well?' She saw his features in the light of a passing car. He had never looked more grave.

'Trust me.'

'What?'

'Just that – keep calm and trust me. We're going for a drive, you and I. And it's not just around the block and back again.'

Shock tore through her as he put the van into gear and drove out of the parking ground. She said weakly, 'You're crazy!'

'It may seem so.'

'But David . . .'

'Briony will look after David.'

'Briony will . . . Mack, what the hell do you mean?'

He was concentrating on making a right turn across the traffic and didn't answer.

6

She tried to open the door on her side but he leaned over and held the handle in a locked position. 'Do you want to kill yourself! Sit still. There's an explanation.'

'Then give it to me.' She was furious.

'Later.'

He pulled the van round into the main stream of traffic and began heading north.

Back at the restaurant Briony returned to the table just as David's exasperation at being kept waiting was beginning to be obvious.

She said shortly, 'I'm sorry. Let's go.'

He explained that the other two had gone out to the van.

'Oh, yes?' She led the way to the main entrance and stood on the top step and looked around her. 'Then we'd better go to your car.'

He was startled. 'What do you mean?'

'The van isn't there any more. Mack has taken your wife for a drive in it.'

'He wouldn't. She wouldn't. You must be mistaken. Where was it parked?'

She indicated one of the empty parking bays. 'Just there.'

He tried to be cool and rational and not let his anger rise. 'He's probably just showing her its paces. They won't be long. Would you like to come back in again for a drink?'

'No.' It was adamant. 'We'll sit in your car.' She knew where it was and made her way over to it. He stopped her as she put her hand on the door-handle.

She looked like a child. A nice child. Not a tart. Was this Mack's idea of a joke. A swop. You take my girl while I have it off with Dee . . . again. Not seriously this time, of course. We'll be back soon. Just long enough to scratch up the old jealousy and make you sweat.

Briony said, 'Please get into the car. The others will be coming out and it won't be easy to get through the exit . . . all the cars.'

He didn't know what she was talking about.

She said, 'Please!' The night air was blowing soft strands of brown hair over her forehead. She was small-boned. Fragile. There was a tremor of panic in her voice.

He got into the driving seat and she got in beside him.

He asked shortly, 'What do you mean – get out of here – why?'

'You'll understand in a minute. Just get out.'

'I'm not leaving here until Mackilroy returns with my wife.'

'Wait until doomsday if you want to – but wait on the other side of the road.'

He thought he detected hysteria and decided to comply. The road outside the restaurant had double yellow lines. He parked on them.

'And now,' she said, 'watch.'

He waited and watched and saw nothing except a London road on a cold Spring night. A restaurant with an adjacent car-park full of cars. Pedestrians. A solitary aeroplane in a cloud-torn sky. The dial of his dashboard clock pointing to ten fifteen – ten twenty – ten twenty-five.

He was aware that her body was hooped over her folded arms in a coil of tension. And then suddenly, like a released spring, she wrenched open the car door and was running across the road between the traffic and making for the restaurant. The main doors opened as she almost reached them and she was caught in the rush and surge of the people as they fled the building. The flash and tulip flare of the explosion quivered the air before the sudden blackness of a rain of dust and debris. Screams mingled with the crash of breaking glass.

Then there was total ear-numbing silence, broken several minutes later by the far-off sounds of approaching sirens.

David, at first not understanding, and then shocked into immobility, was about to get out of the car when she returned to it. She was bleeding from a cut on her cheek and was speaking hoarsely through sobs. 'They mis-timed the warning. Oh, God! Oh, God! Get me out of here . . . please!'

8

He looked at her aghast. 'You . . .?' He couldn't frame the accusation. It was unbelievable.

Her tears were mingling with the blood on her face. 'There was time to clear the building. It should have been cleared. The warning came too late. No one should have been hurt. Please let no one be hurt.'

It was believable. He felt a sick disgust. 'Damn you!'

She leaned over and turned on the ignition. 'Don't just sit there – start the car.'

He was doubly appalled that she should expect him to assist in her get-away. 'You must be out of your mind!'

'Then what are you going to do?'

'Fetch the police. Hand you over. And then see if I can help anyone who didn't get out in time.'

She became aware of the blood on her face and tried to wipe it away with the back of her hand, but it still kept coming. Her panic rose even more. 'How can I stop it?'

He didn't know and he didn't care. He supposed the police would take her to the nearest casualty department . . . along with the rest. He was trembling and his body was bathed with a cold sweat. There was a faint insistent thrumming in his ears as if the explosion was going on and on in the distance and in a minor muted key.

She was regaining control of herself. 'If you fetch the police and hand me over what do you suppose will happen to Dee?'

'What?' He was half way out of the car and remained crouched and still as if frozen in ice. 'What did you say?'

She said in a very tired small voice. 'If you want your wife back alive and well, you'll have to make sure that nothing happens to me.'

'You mean that Mackilroy . . .?' The implication was difficult to take in. His mind tried to do a volte-face and see the situation from a completely different angle.

'Mack – and others – not just Mack.'

Fury broke in him and he took her by the shoulders and shook her. 'Where is she? Where has he taken her? If she's hurt then I'll hurt you, so help me!' The blood from her face was spattering over his hand. Appalled at a violence he didn't know he was capable of he let his hands drop.

She was almost calm now. 'No one need be hurt.' She glanced sideways at the restaurant and then quickly looked away again. 'While I'm all right, Dee will be all right. All we have to do is to go to your Kensington flat and await orders. If the police see us parked here and come over to question you, it will be too late for Dee. Do you understand me? It will be too late for Dee.'

He spoke through thick clouds of fury. 'What am I to do?'

'For a start, drive me to your flat. You've no one staying with you at the moment. No one will know I'm there.'

'And Dee? Where's Dee?'

'Dee will spend the time she's away from you in the country – not far from London, but far enough.' She added surprisingly. 'I'm sorry it had to be Mack. I mean sorry for you. But it's better for Dee that way.' She noticed a clean duster in the glove compartment and wiped the blood from her cheek.

He began driving and relief that he was heeding her made the tears come again. She sat with the duster pressed against her face trying to quell them. He would play along, she thought, he loved his wife too well not to.

Dee knew nothing of the explosion for some time. She believed that the lunatic drive was due to some aberration on Mack's part. He was either drunk or paranoid. She had made several determined efforts to make him stop the van, turn it around and take her back and at last almost viciously he had told her to shut up.

As an abduction it was fast losing its charm and she told him so.

'Had there been time,' he said, 'I could have persuaded you to come willingly.'

She turned that over in her mind and wondered if it were true. Innately honest with herself she believed that it might be. There were times when her life with David seemed to offer her nothing but a succession of days of bored frustration. If they had had a child it would have been better. They had tried and nothing had happened. Constituency work didn't appeal to her. She did it out of a sense of duty. She had always found it difficult to mix with people. Hers wasn't a platform personality. She endured agonies of shyness at public meetings. Worse than anything she despised the cut and thrust of political argument – too often it descended to the level of abuse for the sake of abuse. If David were speaking in the House she went and listened and was proud of him. When the opposition tore down the edifice of his argument, as it frequently did, she felt a sick helplessness and vowed she would never attend again. Her reaction amused him. He knew she wasn't a political animal and never would be, but he appreciated the fact that she played the part as best she could.

Mack pulled the van in at a layby. He had used minor roads once he had left the M4 out of London and she had no idea where she was. The signposts for the past twenty miles had indicated villages she had never heard of and in places the roads had been so little used that grass grew along the crown of them. She watched him switch off the ignition and told him sharply that he had come a long way to bed her down on the back seat. She was mystified and still very angry. If this had happened when David was away from home she might have taken it as the joke it must surely be, but to leave David high and dry and worried back at the restaurant with the girl wasn't funny.

Mack turned on the radio and then put his hand on hers. 'It's the late news. Don't worry about what you're going to hear. David will have left the restaurant at least twenty minutes before it happened.'

He turned up the sound.

The announcer's voice came familiarly over the air. 'The

11

casualty figures of the bombing at the Silver Swan Restaurant have now risen to four killed and approximately twenty injured. A telephoned warning that a bomb had been planted came only three minutes before the explosion and it was impossible to evacuate the building in time. If further news comes in during the bulletin we will keep you informed. In the meantime . . .'

Mack swore and turned the radio off: 'Bloody incompetence! There was time – and to spare. It should have been cleared.'

Dee felt her head swimming. 'You mean – you knew?' It was a nightmare. She couldn't believe it.

He repeated what he had said earlier. 'David is all right. Briony will have got him out. There's a call-box down the road from here. We'll walk to it and I'll wait with you while you phone. It will put your mind at rest. You can't spend the night not knowing.'

She couldn't believe that any of it was happening. He took a torch from his pocket and it spilt a thin trickle of light ahead of them as they walked. Her mind clamoured with questions but she was incapable of asking any of them. He realized she was in a state bordering on shock, but couldn't do anything about it. He hoped Briony had got David out in time. He hoped particularly that Briony had got herself out. The exercise had been planned with meticulous attention to detail. It shouldn't have gone wrong. But it had.

He knew the number of the Kensington flat and dialled it. When he heard the ringing tone he handed the phone to Dee. 'Briony will have told David not to do anything stupid. I'm telling you the same now. Accept what's happening. You have to.'

She took the receiver from him with fingers that were ice cold and then there was David's voice sharp with anxiety, 'Yes? Who is it?'

Tears thickened at the back of her throat so that his name came out slurred. 'David – oh, David!'

There was a moment's silence. 'Dee? For Christ's sake are you all right? Where are you?'

12

She was crying too much with relief that he wasn't hurt to be able to speak. Mack took the phone from her. 'She's just heard the news about the restaurant. She needed to know that you weren't there. Reassure her and then pass the phone to Briony. She's standing beside you, I expect.'

'Oh yes, she's standing beside me.' It was dry.

Dee forced herself to be controlled. She took the receiver again. 'David, I didn't know this was going to happen. I had no part in any of it. I didn't know Mack was coming to the restaurant. I didn't know his intentions when he took me to the van. For God's sake, David, believe me.'

'Of course I believe you.' The fact that he and Dee were caught up in what was becoming one of the hazards of this dangerous decade was beginning to make some impact on him. The circumstances in their case had a bizarre twist. His wife's kidnapper was her former lover and his own was a seven-stone sprat of a girl he could break with one hand tied behind him. She wasn't even armed – just standing there watching him – a plaster on her cheek, her eyes dark with fatigue. Standing there supremely confident that he was unable to do a thing. And of course he wasn't able to do anything. If he overpowered the girl and called the police what would happen to Dee? Perhaps nothing. Perhaps it was just a gigantic bluff. Mack on his own and the girl. But for what purpose?

He didn't believe that Mack was on his own and the purpose he was quite sure would be spelt out quite clearly and concisely in due time.

He knew that Dee was crying. He hadn't heard her cry in years. The most pressing and urgent need was to try to give her some comfort and calm her down. He used his pet name for her, 'Deedee, do you know where you are?'

'No – other than in a call box on a country road. I think Berkshire, or perhaps just into Wiltshire.'

'Well – wherever you are, darling, you're with Mackilroy and he can't mean you any harm.' It had cost him a lot to say that, but he believed it to be true and derived some comfort from it. 'This sort of thing has happened to other people. They've played it quietly and got through safely. Try not to worry. Leave the positive side of things to me.' He wanted to add that he loved her, but Mack had taken the phone from her and was asking for Briony. David swore at him quietly and at length before handing the phone over. Mack listened patiently and without comment. There would be a lot of bitterness before the plan was finally completed, and there would be more bloodshed. He wondered how the four of them would survive the coming weeks.

Dee, back in the road again, felt she wanted to retch. The smell in the phone-box, metallic and dusty, seemed more in keeping with the situation than the sweetness of the country air outside. The night was dark and starless. There was a screech from a small creature in the field followed by the gentle cry of a bird. Mack was giving directions to the girl but he had closed the phone-box door and she couldn't hear clearly what he was saying. She wondered if she should walk away across the fields and into the deeper darkness of a small copse that pencilled the skyline, but she was too troubled to think straight. Walk away from Mack? She had always walked to Mack. He had until now seemed an extension of herself. Flesh of her flesh.

Back in the van she tried to make order out of her chaotic thoughts and began with some basic questions. 'I didn't know you associated with terrorists?'

He noticed she had carefully put him on the perimeter and not called him one. He didn't answer.

'The Provisionals?'

He didn't answer that either.

'Yes – or no?'

'Yes or no – nothing. I'm not discussing it with you.'

Her temper snapped. 'You're not discussing it with me. You

have the gall to force me to come away with you. You knew that a bomb was to go off tonight. People have been killed. Why – for God's sake – why?'

He swung the van down a side road and concentrated on not scraping the hedges. The road was used very rarely and then only by tractors. The van's wheels churned in the mud. The cottage was well chosen. A summer residence for an anti-social couple who would have appreciated Siberia.

He answered her question. 'Why the bomb? As emphasis. It was intended to damage – not kill.'

'But it did kill.'

'Yes.' He had shown remorse earlier. Not now.

He cornered carefully.

'What do you mean – emphasis?'

'It emphasised the seriousness of our intention. Had it not happened do you suppose David would have listened to Briony? He would have laughed at her story and sent her packing.'

'And now?'

'And now he's listening. He'll do as she tells him. He'll know it isn't a game.'

'I see. And what happens if David goes to the police?'

He didn't answer.

She repeated it. 'What happens if David does the sensible, logical thing and tells the police the whole story?'

'He won't.'

'Why not?'

Again he didn't answer.

'Because of what you'll do to me – is that it? On the night of the execution the protagonists made love – is that it? For Christ's sake, this is us. You and I. Are you seriously trying to tell me that if David goes to the police you'll stick a gun in my gut?'

'David won't go to the police. I know him. I know you. If he plays his part sensibly – and he will – you'll be back together very soon.'

'Play his part? What do you want him to do? Allow your dear Briony to set up a bomb factory in the dining-room – is that it? Or a Kensington-based communications room for the IRA or the PLO or whatever misguided group you've thrown in your lot with?' She shook her head like a swimmer emerging from deep water. 'This isn't true. It's a hoax. A stupid, sick joke. The bomb happened – but it had nothing to do with you.'

He said gently, 'It's easier to accept facts than to fight them. Our Group needs David – or more specifically we need his influence. Through you we've got him.'

'I see.' It was bitter. 'It was fortunate you had an affair with the wife of an MP, wasn't it? Even more fortunate that he achieved ministerial rank. You planned far ahead. Congratulations.'

He refused to lose his cool. 'I planned nothing and you know it. You could have left him and come to me. I wanted you.'

'I loved you.'

'And I you.'

'At least now we've got the tense right.'

'Not necessarily.' He switched on the interior light of the van as he brought it to a standstill and then he turned to look at her. Despite her fatigue, her shock, her anger, her attraction burned as strongly as ever for him. 'Not necessarily,' he repeated. 'Not necessarily at all.'

The cottage had basic comforts including electricity and water. There were two bedrooms, a living room and a kitchen. A fire burned low in the grate. Mack noticed it. The others had been and gone as arranged. They had muzzled the dog – also as arranged. It was an airedale, curly-haired, trim, efficient. Mack removed the muzzle and it thumped its tail at him. He said, 'Hey, there. Did you think we were never coming?' He went through to a lean-to and brought back the animal's feeding bowl and a bowl of water. 'His name is Lex,' he told Dee. 'After he's eaten, I'll put him outside. He sleeps in the barn.'

Dee took off her wrap and put it on the back of a chair. The cottage was warm but it smelt musty and old. There was a yellowed oil painting of a mill-stream over the stone fireplace. A red plush sofa with sagging springs was pushed under a small curtained window. On a chipped mahogany table someone had recently left a half-smoked cheroot on a dirty ash-tray.

Mack was stroking the dog as it bolted down its food. His fussing over the animal irritated her. She picked up the cheroot. 'You don't smoke these, do you?'

He glanced over. 'No.'

'Then whose?'

'No one you need bother about.'

'Is he coming back?'

'Not tonight.'

'But sometime?'

'Probably.'

She felt a squirm of fear in her stomach. 'Who are these people? You've got to tell me.'

'The less you know the better.' He went and pushed a poker into the dying fire and raised the coal so that it could have air. And then meticulously he picked out small pieces of coal from the scuttle and built a small pyramid that the flames could lick around. He wondered if she was cold.

'I've brought clothes for you.'

'What?' She was startled.

'Well, you can't spend the next few days in a green evening gown with spangles on it.'

At another time his description of silver thread embroidery on dark green pure silk might have amused her. It had been David's birthday present to match the emerald bracelet. A wedding anniversary and a birthday falling on the same day resulted invariably in a double present. He had always been generous to a fault.

'Go and see them. They're on the bed through there. I had to

17

guess your size. I hope they'll do.'

Briony had offered to get them but he hadn't let her. It had amused him to make the selection himself. The black and white tartan skirt was similar to the one he had remembered her wearing in Scotland. He had teased her about it at the time, calling it a sacrilege on an English lassie who hadn't a drop of Scottish blood in her veins.

In the bedroom Dee looked at it and remembered. Sudden tears burned at the back of her eyes. It was several minutes before she was calm enough and curious enough to look at the rest of the clothes. A couple of sweaters – one blue, one black. A fisherman's knit cardigan – several pairs of tights – espadrilles.

He came to the bedroom door and watched her. 'There's washing gear on the bedside table. Your favourite talc.' He didn't mention the tampons but she noticed them. They wouldn't be needed for another couple of weeks and pray God she'd be out of the place by then.

'Have I forgotten anything?'

'Nightwear.'

'You don't wear any.'

'It was summertime – then . . .'

He went over and touched her cheek with the back of his hand. She moved away from him.

'Dee?'

'No.'

'Please . . .'

'No.'

He knew she was remembering the bomb.

He went quickly out of the bedroom and closed the door behind him. There would be other nights. There was plenty of time.

TWO

Briony said, 'You're wasting your time preaching at me – and trying to tag labels on me. I'm not intelligent. I can't argue about ideologies with you. I do what I feel I must do. I'm part of the Group because I feel I must be part of it. It's not for me to give you details of it – someone else will . . . later. If I were allowed to – and I'm not – you'd shred it – premise by premise. You'd emphasize the violence and make nonsense of the cause.'

She was sitting opposite him in the big brown leather chair in the study. Her legs were inelegantly tucked under her and her shoes were scuffing the brown velvet cushion. The intervening hours – plus a liberal supply of David's whisky – had calmed her. Conversation, uneasy at first, had become possible.

David had his own emotions well under control. 'Any belief that is based on murder and violence ends murderously and violently.'

'Not always. Can you tell me of any continuing faith or dogma that hasn't spilt blood somewhere along the line?'

'You're trying to salve your conscience with talk. The bombing happened. You caused it. People have died.'

He saw with satisfaction that she winced.

'Yes, people have died. It wasn't intended.'

'That doesn't make it unhappen.'

She looked at her empty glass. 'May I have more of your whisky? If we're to sit here and talk all night it will help me to be articulate.

19

When I'm stone cold sober my tongue goes to sleep in my mouth.'

He got up and poured her a full measure. He remembered that she had drunk shandy before the explosion. Obviously she was being careful then. Now reaction was kicking out the caution. In time, perhaps, she'd tell him everything he needed to know.

'How old are you, Briony?' The question had passed his lips almost before he knew he was going to ask it.

'Twenty-four. Does that make you feel better? I know I don't look it. Twenty-four – the age of reason plus – plus – plus. What more do you want to know? Where I was born? Birmingham. Do you believe me? It doesn't matter. My parents? Second generation Italian with good old Brummy accents. I haven't seen them for years. Sort out what you want to believe from that lot and then tell me if you want any more.' She was very pale.

'Does your cheek still pain you?'

She reached up and touched the dressing. 'Is the blood coming through?'

'No.'

'Yes, it still pains. It's a fair retribution, isn't it? Only to be fairer it should have been worse. I should have had my head blown off.' She added almost to herself. 'At least I went back. I tried.'

He had to concede that. A cold-blooded act followed by an emotional reaction.

'Yes, you went back. You needn't have done.'

'It was stupid of me. Had I been killed it would have ruined the whole thing.'

'Until the next time. With other operatives. Tell me about Mackilroy.'

'You tell me. You knew him all those years ago.'

'So he told you about that, too?' He managed to get it out evenly, displaying no feeling at all.

'Just the facts. He filled the gap for Dee when you were recalled to London. It began as an amusement but finished as something

20

more. You nearly split up over it. Why didn't you? Because of your career?'

He had no intention of submitting to an analysis of his marriage. They stayed together because he loved Dee beyond pain or pride or any other emotion. And she had stayed with him without coercion for reasons he had never probed.

'We were talking about Mackilroy.'

She sipped her whisky. 'Can you separate the two? Did you notice her face when we came across the restaurant?'

It was cruel, but he let it bounce off him.

'How long have you known him, Briony?'

'Long enough. Not as long as you in actual time. But long enough. Irish Scottish ancestry. What does that make him? An Irish Nationalist? A Scottish Nationalist? There might even be a little Welsh somewhere. Shall we throw that in for good measure? He's been out in Israel, too, you know. And the Arab States. Freelance journalism gets one around. One gets involved. No, David, I'm not going to tell you anything. Even if I drink your whisky until I'm soaked I still won't tell you a thing.'

The French carriage clock was ticking softly, busily in the silence. To the side of it was a portrait of Dee, her lips faintly smiling as if she could see them and was amused. The two women couldn't be more different. Dee, high cheekboned, dark eyed, with a natural grace of movement that would in time turn beauty into elegance. Briony, small, brown, mouse-like but with a will like a tiger that shone through heavily lashed green eyes.

She yawned. 'I don't know for how long you and I are going to be incarcerated together, but if we're to sit up in these damned chairs night after night we're not going to be worth much at the end of it.'

'There's a spare bedroom down the corridor on the left. Use it if you want to.'

'And you – what are you going to do?'

21

'There's the front door and there's the telephone. I might decide to use one or the other. I don't know.'

She yawned again. 'I wouldn't advise it. Go out if you want to. If you do, you'll be tailed. Not by me. There are others. Use the phone if you wish. It's bugged. Do one or the other and you won't get Dee back.'

'I can't seriously believe that Mack would hurt her.'

'Oh no, Mack won't hurt her – not unless he has to – and then he'll get someone else to do it for him. Don't judge him by your own standards.' She looked at him thoughtfully. 'Or yes – perhaps – do. Earlier this evening you would have happily seen me dead. There's a core of violence in everyone. In you. In Mack. I don't know how far he'd go – but then neither do you. If you love your wife you won't test him.'

She uncoiled herself from the chair and stood up stretching.

'May I help myself to a glass of milk before I go to bed?'

'There's some in the fridge.'

She hesitated. 'I know I don't fit the category of a weekend guest, but I could do with a dressing-gown. Is Dee's sacrosanct?'

He had noticed the hesitation otherwise he would have told her to go to the devil. 'You'll find one in the wardrobe in the spare room.'

She said quite seriously, 'You are immensely civilized.'

He answered with a depth of irony that was quite lost on her, 'Thanks.'

After she had left the room he tried to drum up some constructive thinking. It was difficult to be objective, but he tried to be. If Dee were to be returned for money then the transaction would be reasonably straightforward, but he doubted if she had been taken for that reason. Wealth was comparative. He had enough. He was, to use the current phrase, comfortable. But he certainly hadn't enough to justify a kidnapping. So – what else did they want? As Defence Minister he had access to classified material. Was that it? The possibility worried him deeply. But why choose him? There were other less obvious people with similar access and less power of retaliation.

Perhaps it was after all just a macabre hoax. Perhaps at this moment Dee and Mack were lying in each other's arms and laughing at him for the fool he undoubtedly was. He killed the thought as soon as it formed. Dee's distress had come clearly over the phone. It hadn't been simulated. The bomb wasn't a hoax.

Mackilroy's part in the affair was difficult to understand. His Irish background made it likely that he was involved with the Provisionals and intended using Dee as a lever to negotiate for the release or transfer to Ireland of prisoners held in this country. He had never in conversation appeared particularly involved in Irish politics. During the conversation earlier in the evening he had not appeared in any way committed. But, of course, he wouldn't have made it obvious.

Briony's warning about not going out or using the phone might be bluff, but he had a strong feeling it wasn't. He went over to the phone and examined it. There was nothing obviously different about it. Instinct told him to put it down. The bombing of the Silver Swan was a measure of the seriousness of the situation. Whoever was responsible, apart from Briony and Mackilroy, wouldn't go to these lengths and then give him freedom to phone the police.

The flat was on the ground floor and had its own separate entrance. He went to the front door and looked up and down the road. It was after two o'clock in the morning but there were people around and there were lights in several windows. That wasn't unusual. He had an uncomfortable feeling that he was framed in the lighted doorway and was being watched. That, too, wasn't unusual. The mind was quick to believe what it was told to believe.

If Dee were not with Mackilroy he would have taken a chance and gone for help. But Dee was with Mackilroy . . . and they had once been lovers. This time he didn't kill the thought so quickly. If

23

the police burst in on Dee and Mackilroy and they were in bed together . . .

He closed the door and went back into the flat.

Briony had needed several stiff drinks to find a degree of calm. Her drinking had made her verbose, but she had given nothing away apart from the fact that she worked for a group. For the first time that night he poured himself a whisky and took it over to the desk. Hatred of Mackilroy was like a tumour that had lain quiescent for a long time but had now taken on a new malignancy. The whisky helped to dull the feeling a little. He took a piece of paper from the desk and on it made a list of all the subversive groups known to be operating in Britain. He made an analysis of their aims and then tried to equate them with the present situation. Nothing was clear-cut. Anything was possible.

He realized that he was very tired and that his brain wasn't functioning clearly. It was after three and it was pointless to stay up any longer. Nothing could be done tonight.

He passed the spare bedroom on the way to his own and felt the draught from the open window cutting across the corridor. He paused by the door and looked in. Briony was leaning against the wall by the window. The small bedside lamp caught her in a pool of light and he saw that she was having difficulty with her breathing.

He hadn't seen an asthmatical attack before but guessed that this was one and didn't know what to do. He stood looking at her helplessly as she fought to get her breath.

She said through blue lips – 'Better . . . soon . . .'

'How can I help?'

'No . . . way . . .'

'A hot drink?'

'No . . .'

She went on heaving and shuddering and his own nerves seemed to explode. 'I'll phone for a doctor.'

'No . . . no . . . no . . .'

He watched and waited helplessly and at last the attack was over. She threw herself on the bed in a storm of tears. 'I didn't mean them to die. Dear God, I didn't mean them to die. Dear God, help me. I don't know what to do.'

He put his hand on her hair and she turned over and grasped it and pressed it against her face. Her teeth were on his knuckles as she sobbed open-mouthed like a child. 'I had a dream – I kept seeing them – there was blood – and a mortuary – and a child with no arms and I couldn't breathe – I couldn't breathe – oh, God, I wish I'd died there, too.'

He said prosaically, 'There was no mention of a child being killed. There were no children there.'

'But you don't know . . . my dream . . .'

'According to the news bulletin four people died. No child was mentioned.'

'And is that supposed to help me? Four people died. Tell me it didn't happen. Tell me I didn't do it.'

She looked up at him grey-faced and pushed his hand away. 'Don't look at me like that. Oh, God, David, try to give me some comfort.'

He said quietly, 'It happened. What else can I say to you?'

'I have never killed before. I have never even seen anyone dead.'

He believed her. It would help her conscience if she went to the police now, but it wouldn't help the dead . . . and he didn't know what it would do for Dee.

The duvet had fallen on the floor and he picked it up. 'Get under this. You're as cold as ice. Can you breathe properly now if I close the window?'

She got into bed and pulled the duvet up around her. 'Yes, I think so.'

'I'll fetch you a hotwater bottle.'

'No. Don't leave the room. I'm afraid to dream again. Don't go.'

25

He stood and looked down at her. Why should he stay and comfort her – why should her asthma and her tears and her contrition get under his skin so that he could forget everything she was and had done? She lay hunched up on the pillows, her face blotched with tears and her hair a tangle over her eyes. She was unattractive in her grief, like a waif picked up out of the gutter.

And he suddenly wanted her – unexpectedly and very strongly – and she knew it.

He turned from her abruptly and left the room.

The morning papers arrived shortly after seven o'clock. *The Times* and *The Telegraph* gave front page coverage to the bombing. The accounts were factual and the pictures not particularly harrowing. David wished he could get at some of the more lurid dailies and drop them in Briony's lap one by one. Any sympathy he had felt for her the night before had been dissipated.

He heard her go through into the kitchen and followed her.

She was making coffee and having difficulty with the percolator. 'How does this work? I'm not good on contraptions.' Her back was to him.

'Good enough at setting a timing device on a bomb.'

'Oh, I see,' she half turned to him, 'we're back behind enemy lines again.' She noticed the newspapers where he had put them on the kitchen table and then averted her gaze. 'I didn't set the timing device.'

'But you planted the bomb. When you left the restaurant you fetched it from the van, that is so, isn't it?'

She didn't answer.

'Shall I read you the newspaper accounts – or will you read them yourself?'

She left the percolator to him and began making toast. Her actions were clumsy. 'What good will it do?'

'To the dead – none.'

'Last night you were kind.'

26

He went over and sat at the table. 'Come on, Briony, read. Find out what you've done. One of the injured lost a leg – another lost an eye. That's the sort of thing that happens when there's an explosion in a confined area. What did you expect would happen – a few shredded table cloths – a hole in the carpet?'

'The restaurant was to have been cleared.'

'But it wasn't, was it? High explosives are unpredictable. How many unpredictable bombs causing how many unpredictable deaths have you been responsible for?'

'It was my first. I told you last night that I hadn't killed before. You believed me then. Why disbelieve me now?'

He poured out some coffee for himself. She waited and then shrugging slightly went to fetch her own.

'So what are you going to do, David?'

He had been thinking about it. 'There's just the two of us here.'

She nodded, understanding perfectly, 'Yes.'

'I could force you to tell me where Mackilroy has taken my wife.'

'Quite easily.' She looked at him over the rim of the coffee cup. 'And what method would you use? A beating up? Cigarette burns? That kitchen knife over there at my throat? I think you could have done any of those things in the car last night – just after the explosion. But can you do them now on this nice Spring morning – in this pretty blue and white kitchen? It's not easy to be brutal on demand – not unless you have that sort of mentality. And you haven't, have you? You're a prisoner of your upbringing and you won't break out of your cage all that easily.'

'Be careful not to assume too much.'

She bit into a piece of toast. 'I'm just pointing out what I believe to be true. Last night my asthma upset you. It made you protective. Many a man under those circumstances would have been happy to see me choke to death. You looked as if you were ready to choke to death yourself in sympathy.' She smiled wryly. 'I like you. It's as well, isn't it, that I do.'

27

'You won't tell me of your own volition where my wife is?'

'Other than that she's in a cottage in Wiltshire – no.'

'Do you know the exact location of the cottage?'

'No. Mack wouldn't have been fool enough to tell me. Mack can get any information he wants out of anybody – man or woman – in five seconds flat. And I'm not saying that with any admiration. We're colleagues – he and I. There's no affection between us. Dee thinks there is. She ground me between her teeth into small bits when she saw me with him in the restaurant last night. She needn't have bothered. He's not for me.'

The kitchen clock struck eight. They both looked up at it.

Briony said, 'You won't be going to work today, of course. Or am I using the wrong word? Your Constituency – the House – the Department – or wherever place you do your daily grind. You'd better phone whoever is expecting you and say you're sick.'

The situation, David thought, was getting out of his control. She sat there, all seven stone of her, and dictated to him like a small, indomitable Genghis Khan.

He regained the initiative. 'Who bugged the phone?'

She shrugged. 'Does it matter?'

'Yes, if you're to convince me that it's bugged at all, I want details.'

'Very well – you shall have them. Dee did her good works – library trolley, isn't it – at the hospital last Wednesday afternoon. The flat was entered through the pantry window. There's a faulty catch. Your phone was attended to. I don't know how, I told you I'm no good with contraptions. One of the flats across the road had new tenants a month ago. They'll know if you phone the police. They'll know if you take a walk outside the flat. They know the precise location of the cottage. They're not squeamish about bombs – or firearms – or death. Don't go looking for trouble, David. Make your phone call to your secretary and then sit back and wait. You'll be contacted. You'll be told what to do.'

28

He had to accept the inevitable. If his anxiety for Dee were not so intense he could accept it with a degree of calm.

While he was in his study making the phone call Briony read the two accounts of the bombings. They were as bad as she feared they would be. She pushed the papers away from her and went upstairs to the bathroom and locked the door. She felt sick and her breathing was worrying her again. She rested her forehead against the wall tiles and took long deep breaths. It was a pity, she thought bitterly, that the Group didn't know of this particular physical weakness. If they had they would never have given her this assignment. They believed her to be both physically and emotionally tough – as she had believed herself to be. She hadn't had an asthmatical attack in years until last night.

Last night.

Last night David had wanted to sleep with her. His hostility this morning stemmed partly from a sense of guilt that he had wanted to sleep with her. It had been a two pronged attack. One against her act of terrorism. The other against herself. Understanding his reaction didn't make it any easier. She wished she could see as clearly into her own mind.

David, not a facile liar, made his excuse for his absence as convincing as he could and hoped he would be believed. His secretary, Alex Pruet, offered to bring some papers around immediately for signature.

He refused emphatically, 'I'm leaving the flat at once – a family crisis.'

'And you don't know when you'll return?'

'I'll contact you when I do.'

Pruet's plummy voice was anxious. 'Can you give me a number where I can reach you, sir?'

'No.' A request for an address would come next. 'I'm sorry, Alex, but I don't envisage anything turning up that can't be handled.' He would have done better to have been flat on his back

29

with flu, but he didn't think he could have simulated a voice sick enough to fit, anyway it was too late now. He said abruptly that he had to be off, and put the phone down.

It was odd to think that not so long ago he had believed himself to be indispensable. If Dee were here with him he could almost enjoy the situation. For the first time in his life – or at any rate for many years – he was being forced into inactivity. God knew what the next few hours would bring, but in the meantime he had damn all to do except sit and wait. He decided to do *The Times* crossword puzzle.

Briony came in and sat opposite watching him. He noticed that she had put a fresh plaster on her cheek. He also noticed a small nervous tic at the corner of her mouth. There was a long silence and she was the first to break it.

'Talk to me.'

He glanced up. 'About what?'

'Anything.'

'All right – you – Mackilroy – the others. I have to know sometime. Tell me now.'

'I can't.'

He returned to the crossword.

She got up and began to pace the room, stopping at the bookcase. She selected a book of poetry, skimmed through one or two pages, and then flung it aside.

'David.'

'Yes?'

'There are degrees of blindness. He might not be totally blind.'

He replied without looking at her, 'The paper stated he lost an eye.'

'One eye. That's not total blindness.'

He was silent.

'May I have some of your whisky?'

'What – at this hour of the morning?'

30

'Is there any law forbidding me to drink whisky at this hour of the morning?'

'No – help yourself, you know where it is.'

She went over to the drinks cabinet and poured herself a generous measure of Scotch. 'Do you want some?'

'No.'

'What clue are you frowning over?'

'I've got it – aspergillum.' He wrote it down.

She had never heard of it. There was another long silence.

'David.'

'What now?' He pencilled in the final clue and put the paper on the table beside him.

The words came out in a short sharp burst. 'I can't bear just sitting here looking at you and listening to that damnable clock and thinking.'

'You surely to God don't expect me to entertain you!' The smile he gave her was bitter.

'You could play chess with me. Do you play chess?'

'Yes. But not with you. Not now.'

She gave up trying. 'Do you want me to make lunch for us?'

'If I can trust you not to put arsenic in it.'

She gave him a small twist of a smile, and noticed his own lips relax a little. 'It's odd, isn't it,' she said, 'that you have to try so hard to hate me.'

THREE

Dee awoke to a day full of bright Spring sunshine and an insistent clamouring of birds. She pushed open the bedroom window and smelt the sweetness of the morning. The landscape flowed into the skyline like a gently undulating sea. Memory of the previous night was veiled by recent sleep. It hadn't yet acquired sharpness, but when at last it did, it came all the more sharply for being tardy.

She dressed hastily and went into the kitchen. 'Mack!'

He wasn't there.

The kitchen door was open and a couple of robins were quarrelling vociferously on the doorstep. They tumbled and pecked and feathers flew. She clapped her hands at them and they tore themselves apart reluctantly and flew into a blackthorn bush. Bright, shiny, young leaves crackled on twigs.

It took her a couple of minutes to search the cottage. The other bedroom, as dreary as her own, was empty. The bed had been untidily made and there was a rucksack on the floor beside it. She went through the rucksack and found it contained a couple of clean shirts, some shaving cream, and a colour print of herself in a leather frame. It had been taken during the early part of the Scottish holiday by David and she had sent it to Mack when she had finally decided to stay with David. He hadn't acknowledged it. In time she had come to accept the break between them as absolute. An island in time on which to build dreams was, she had believed, better than

33

nothing. It was somewhere to escape to in her mind when her own petal-hatted image of herself was getting too hard to bear. Now Mack had exploded that island as neatly as if he had planted the bomb right in the middle of it.

It was extraordinary, she thought, how one could love a person and yet not know him at all. What had they talked about all those years ago? She tried to recall any strongly held views he might have had and couldn't come up with a single one. Religion hadn't played any part in his life. Political discussions had been too much David's sphere and reminded them too much of David. Nationalism was almost part and parcel of the same thing. As a journalist he had seemed to her more an observer than a participator. He went, he saw, he recorded. As far as she knew at that particular time he hadn't given a damn. His objectivity had been like a cold refreshing bath compared with David's total absorption. David, a Minister of the Crown, was a natural sequel to David the committed representative of a sprawling hard-speaking multiracial community with as many colours as a Joseph's coat and with creeds to match. With his public school background followed by Oxford and with generations of pedantic forebears to shape his genes he should have been a misfit in the constituency. That he wasn't was due to the strength and honesty of his commitment. He cared and his constituents knew it.

Mack, too, obviously cared about something and cared brutally and destructively. Thinking back over the evening, Briony must have been planting the bomb at the time when David was giving an account of the Greek holiday and Mack was listening with grudging amusement, totally calm.

Briony.

Briony, Mack said, would look after David. It was clear from the phone call of last night that Briony was looking after David in the Kensington flat. It shouldn't tax his ingenuity too much to get rid of her. Come to that, it shouldn't tax her own ingenuity to walk out of this empty cottage now, find a main road somewhere at the bottom of the cart-track and thumb a lift back to town.

She took Mack's rucksack and stuffed her evening gown into it together with a couple of bread rolls from the bread bin in the kitchen and a wedge of cheese. A sketchy wash under the tap was better than nothing and a drink of milk, though not very palatable as it was yesterday's and not refrigerated, was quicker than making tea. It seemed better not to loiter, though as far as she could tell there was no one in the vicinity.

The cottage had no garden, just a small brick path that meandered hopefully for a few yards and then lost itself in the tall springing grasses. The cart track widened into a semi-circular parking space and there were tyre marks where the van had stood last night. It wasn't there now.

She had walked less than a hundred yards down the track when the dog appeared. It came slowly on its belly from the obscurity of the high grass in the untamed field. It growled softly, its black lips arching stiffly over menacing teeth. No longer the mild creature of the night before that Mack had fondled, it inched closer daring her to move.

Ram-rod stiff with fright, she felt as if she had been cast in stone. The dog, five yards away now, circled her, still crouching, its shoulder muscles rippling under its hair.

When it was almost in snapping distance it halted directly in front of her, its amber eyes almost human in their command that she should take a step backward – and then another – and another – in the direction of the cottage. As terrified as a stray sheep she retraced her steps, her eyes riveted on the dog's. It wasn't until she was over the threshold that the animal relaxed. As if motivated by electrical energy that was suddenly cut off, it flopped limply across the step.

When Mack returned with the van just after eleven o'clock it had taken itself off to the fields again. Dee, unable to see it but acutely aware that it was there, sat within slamming distance of the

35

door should it decide to try to come in.

She was intensely angry.

Mack, feeling her mood like a slap in the face, guessed the reason for it. He emptied a brown paper bag full of provisions onto the table.

'Did you try to take a walk?'

'You know too damned well I tried to take a walk.'

'Don't do it again. The animal is biddable. He answers to my authority – and to one or two others. He has a job to do.'

Her anger exploded. 'To guard me? To make me stay here? To tear my throat out if I don't? For pity's sake, what's the matter with you? What the hell has gone wrong with you? What are you trying to do?'

He unpacked two pork chops and some meat for the dog. It would be tactful, he thought, to feed the dog in the barn rather than in the house. The barn was in the field at the back of the cottage and housed transmitting equipment. It also housed rats which the dog should have caught, but didn't. Traps had to be set regularly in case they got at the wiring.

After feeding the dog he took a sack of potatoes from the back of the van together with a cross-section of the daily newspapers. He took the potatoes through to the vegetable rack in the kitchen and gave Dee the papers in passing.

She read the accounts of the bombing stonily. The plain fact that a bomb had been set off was difficult enough to digest – in relation to him. Why he should thrust the trimmings of minute details at her was something she couldn't understand.

She passed the papers back to him after about twenty minutes of concentrated reading. 'Well – what do I do now? Applaud you?'

He was peeling potatoes wastefully letting thick spirals of peel fall onto the table top.

'No. Accept something that has happened. Accept the fact that there was a blunder and that people were killed.'

She searched for the word he had used last night. Emphasis. Emphasis of intent. A bomb had been planted so that David should take the girl Briony seriously. At best it was extreme lunacy. At worst . . . as yet she didn't know the worst and it defied her imagination.

She looked at him critically. His long craggy face under the thatch of black hair looked tired and there were hollows under his cheekbones. The face of a fanatic? The face of a man she had once loved to distraction and mourned because he had come into her life too late.

She said aloud, startled by the thought, 'We might have married.'

He missed the nuance. 'The decision was yours. You could have persuaded David to divorce you.'

Yes, she could have persuaded David. He would have fought to hold her, but only for a while. His pain threshold was low. He wouldn't have held her unwillingly. She must have had some deep unacknowledged need to be with him and he must have sensed it. They couldn't have started rebuilding their lives together on nothing. His love for her wouldn't have been enough on its own. No matter how quiet the answering chord in her it must have been there, heard dimly by both of them.

'What's happening to David now?' She couldn't hide the anxiety in her voice.

'He's sitting it out with Briony as you're sitting it out with me.'

'For what purpose?'

It was called softening up. As each hour went by uncertainty would tauten the nerves. Acquiescence would come more easily after time had eroded confidence. The plan depended on complete obedience.

'You'll both be visited. Perhaps sometime today – perhaps tomorrow. I don't know.'

'By whom?'

'One of the Group.'

37

'What group?'

'You'll find out later.'

She drew one of the newspapers to her and read the account again. The police weren't sure who had phoned the warning. The special code number of the Provisionals hadn't been given.

She pointed out the relevant paragraph to him. 'Why didn't you give it?'

'I had nothing to do with the warning. If I had it would have been given in time.'

'And you would have given the number?'

'No.'

'Why not?'

'Because I don't know it.'

'Because you're not a member of the IRA?'

'I didn't say that.'

'But it's true.'

He didn't deny it.

'Then you're on the other side.'

'If you want to think so.'

And that was a denial, too. She knew him well enough to sort the truth out of prevarication. 'Then what is your . . .' this time she used the capital letter in her mind 'Group?'

'I'm not free to tell you yet.'

She gave up and watched him as he put the potatoes on the cooker and the chops under the grill. It was a domesticated scene that hadn't the slightest degree of serenity about it.

'Tell me about Briony.'

He considered the question and then answered it. 'She's been a Group member for some time – a committed one. She's your original ice-cold maiden. I've never seen her show any emotion at all.'

'Are you saying that to console me?'

Her interpretation surprised him. He hadn't seriously thought

38

she would be bothered either way.

'No, I'm just stating a fact.'

She accepted it. 'Does your Group want money from David?'

'No.'

'Then what does it want? What is there so particular about David that you're doing this to the two of us?'

'You'll be told. But not by me.'

Beyond that he refused to go.

After they had eaten a sketchy lunch he suggested she might like to walk with him in the field. Noticing that her fear of the dog still lingered, he called the animal to heel and demonstrated its complete obedience to him. The rapport between him and the animal didn't make her feel any easier. The fact that he was fond of a creature so vicious was hard to take. He agreed reluctantly to send it back to the cottage while they took their walk together.

'Aren't you afraid I'll get too familiar with the lie of the land?' She felt she couldn't converse with him, just make short bitter conversational jabs.

He accepted her attitude, believing it wouldn't last. 'It's just as well that you should. There isn't another house within miles. Lex has been trained not to allow you down the track. As you see, if we go up this way it's just a vast area of uncultivated land.'

'And how far will Lex allow me to go up this way if I decide to come on my own?'

'I don't know and I wouldn't advise you to test him.'

The fields were thick with spring flowers. Buttercups yellowed the hem of her tartan skirt as she brushed past them. Daisies trampled underfoot made a white carpet of crushed petals. They had more than once in the early days of their loving made love in the transient privacy of the Scottish hills. He had been accomplished in his love-making, gentle in his dominance, understanding her as completely as she believed she understood him. Later, when her guilt almost swamped her with remorse and she could talk of no-one but David, he had listened and helped her into a calmer state of mind.

She said, 'We've gone a long way.'

He didn't understand that she spoke of an emotional distance. 'Not so far.'

'I mean from the old days – from each other.'

There was less bitterness now, more a deep distress. He was careful not to assume too much – not to hurry her. The antagonism, born of shock, was still very deep.

'Sit for a while.' The grass was damp from recent April rain and he put his jacket down for the two of them.

She sat miserably, too conscious of him, being careful not to touch him, hoping he wouldn't touch her. She would have given anything at that moment to have put her hand in David's – to have felt his cool firm skin – to have looked deeply into his ordinary, kindly face – to have spoken of normal, ordinary things with him.

'You're very quiet, Dee.'

'I'm missing David.'

He accepted that and wondered how much a true barrier it was. She had thrown up the name often enough in the past; it was part of her defence mechanism – against him – against her natural inclinations.

'How worried do you suppose he is?' She couldn't keep the concern out of her voice.

Probably not particularly worried yet, Mack thought, but hopefully he would be extremely worried in time.

He shrugged and didn't answer.

A period of complete inactivity could, David discovered, change from the quietness of a windless sea to the uneasy stillness of the eye of a hurricane. The changes with some happened more quickly than with others. Though his nerves towards the end of the day were beginning to be rubbed raw he wasn't as far gone as Briony. She couldn't sit still and her constant pacing, intended to get his attention, was getting it.

They had agreed that as he was supposed to be away from the flat the two main rooms, the sitting room and the dining room, which faced the front shouldn't be used. The study was comfortable but small and confining. He had often wondered when he would have time to read the many leather-bound volumes on the shelves, but now that he was given the time he hadn't the inclination. His eyes registered the words but his brain was off on a safari on its own as he turned the pages. The lion country his thoughts wandered through wasn't conducive to calm.

He told Briony irritably to sit down.

'I can't just sit and look at you.'

'Then read.'

'You're not reading.'

He admitted it. 'That's hardly surprising under the circumstances.'

'Then stop pretending.'

He gave her a long critical look, 'What possessed you to get in with the mob in the first place?'

'They're not a mob. We call ourselves the Group.'

'Use whatever name you want to, but answer my question.'

Surprisingly she did. 'My father was killed by a hit and run driver. He was walking home from the local pub.'

'In Birmingham?'

'No, in Woking.'

'You told me Birmingham before – Italian with strong Brummy accents, remember?'

'I told you to believe what you wanted to believe.'

'And what am I to believe now?'

'What I'm telling you now. He was killed and left there.'

He couldn't see any connection but hoped he might in time. 'Well, go on – what happened then?'

41

'Nothing for a long time – and then I joined the Group.'

'What do they do – specialize in orphans? Was your mother killed, too?'

'No. I don't want to talk about it.'

'But you joined the Group as a direct result of your father's death?'

'Yes.'

She shuffled uncomfortably, obviously afraid of giving too much away. 'If you're going to ask me why, then don't because I can't tell you.'

It occurred to him that if he were running a Group – or even a Sunday School – he wouldn't allow her within shouting distance of it. To be a success one had to pick one's team well. He had always been careful to do that. One weak brick and the whole edifice crumbled. Hopefully her nerve would snap soon and she would tell him everything.

Aware of her weakness, she swung into the attack. She had been told to needle him, to use this waiting time positively. 'Dee has been gone nearly twenty-four hours.'

'Yes.' Mentally, he put up the barricades.

'How do you suppose she's taking it?'

'You know the circumstances better than I do.'

'But you know Dee.'

Up to a point, he thought. Loving and knowing were two different things. He didn't answer.

She lunged in with, 'Do you suppose she's sleeping with Mack?', and when that didn't draw a response either, 'It would be odd if they didn't resume the old relationship, wouldn't it?'

He told her quietly to shut up.

She grinned at him, pleased she had drawn blood.

She went over to Dee's portrait and recited in a teasing monotone. 'Dee Berringer, née Deidre Mansfield, twenty-five years old. Daughter of Alan Mansfield, solicitor of Cheltenham and of

Margaretta Mansfield. Educated at Chorley House, a small private
school for girls. At eighteen was secretary to David Berringer, MP.
Married him at twenty. At twenty-two when on holiday in Scotland
met Jack Mackilroy, a freelance journalist, and became his lover.
The affair lasted for precisely thirteen months.' She stopped, trying
to assess the degree of his anger, but he was looking back at her
levelly, giving nothing away.

'You're well-briefed.'

She nodded. 'Oh, yes. The information we have about you both
would surprise you.'

He was quite sure that was true. He had thought that Dee and
Mack had been meeting for nine or ten months at the most. Thirteen
months was probably correct. He had no reason to dispute it.

'That's all in the past.'

'It was,' she pointed out, 'until now.'

'If that's the only basis for the exercise – then aren't you being
rather naive?'

'We would be if it were – but it's not. We want you – not Dee.
She's the hostage to force your hand. Whether or not she chooses
to sleep with Mack while she's being held doesn't matter a damn to
us. She'd be wise to take her fun while she can get it.'

The threat was implicit.

'Meaning that if I don't comply she'll be hurt?'

She noticed the narrowing of his eyes as he fought to retain his
composure. 'That's nothing to do with me.'

The quick nervous back-down wasn't lost to him.

'Of course it's to do with you. You joined your so-called Group.
You either stay with it and accept all responsibility – or you quit.
Your bomb killed and maimed people. Your responsibility. If my
wife is murdered, that's your responsibility, too. If your conscience
is bothering you as much as I think it is then go and sit down over
there now and give me all the information you know so that I can
go to the police with enough evidence for them to act before the –

43

the Group – know what's happening to them.'

'My conscience? My conscience is very well, thank you.' Her voice was taut. 'And even if it were not, I don't know where Dee is being held, I told you that before. If you did go to the police they wouldn't find her in time. If I sabotaged my part of the exercise what difference do you suppose it would make to the plan as a whole? Damn all. Do you think you're dealing with fools? As Minister of Defence do you tell your junior staff every last detail of everything that goes on so that they can blow the gaff either in bed or under pressure or just for sheer bloody-mindedness? You're not dealing with idiots.'

'My position as Minister of Defence – is that what this is all about? What does your mob want – classified information?'

'If they did they'd use other sources – it's nothing to do with that.'

He pounced on it. 'Good. Now we're getting somewhere. What else shall we eliminate? What else isn't it?'

'Play chess with me.'

'What else isn't it?'

'I'll get the board. Where do you keep the chessmen?' She began looking, her movements agitated.

'Go on, Briony, tell me. Use what little vestige of commonsense you have and opt out of the bloody business while there's still time.'

She turned to him. 'Time? Don't kid yourself there's time. For you – for me – for anyone. There's been time – too much time – and what have we done with it?'

He didn't understand and waited hoping for more.

She stood and looked at him. 'You Parliamentarians – you make history, don't you – for good or for bad. You wouldn't be where you are if you weren't power-minded. What sort of thrust pushed you into leadership in the first place – apart from the power aspect? What did you hope to do?'

It seemed to him a digression and he answered it briefly. 'To be a man of the people, I suppose. To represent them. To work for them.'

'To lead them like Moses out of the desert?'

He grinned slightly. 'You sound as if you've been at my whisky again.'

She retorted unsmilingly. 'Idealism is all very well, but if you don't get blood on your banner now and then you might as well fold it up and put it in a drawer.' She saw the box of chessmen on the bureau. 'And now will you play with me?'

'You're a strange girl, Briony. You would have been a tremendous asset to my electioneering. What a pity you weren't around at the right time.' Intended sarcastically it nevertheless had a ring of truth. Dee's scarcely veiled boredom hadn't done much to add to his votes. She had sat at his side and looked pretty and that had been the sum total of it. This girl had a fiery conviction allied to a neat turn of phrase. Had she been batting on the right side she would have been a force to reckon with. Even batting on the wrong side she wouldn't be easy to break. He wondered how long it would take him.

She was setting out the pieces on the board. 'You will play with me, won't you?'

He pulled his chair up to the table. 'What sort of an opponent are you?'

'At least equal to you.'

'Perhaps. We'll see.' He waited for her to make the first move.

She played with less than her usual skill, but even so the game lasted nearly an hour before he called check-mate. Exhausted, but afraid of her thoughts in the darkness of the bedroom, she suggested another game. He declined. 'It's late. I'll sit up awhile.'

'No one will contact you tonight.'

'Then when?'

'I don't know. Perhaps tomorrow.'

He didn't relish the hours of darkness any more than she did.

45

'If you won't play another game, David, then I'll sit up with you.'

'Do as you like.'

Within five minutes she was asleep in the chair. He went through to the darkened sitting room for a cushion and then went over to the window and looked up at the flats opposite. If there were watchers then they weren't to be seen. He had to take a lot on trust. He didn't dare do otherwise. He returned to the study with the cushion and put it behind her head.

She awoke sometime later when he was asleep. The lines of strain in his face were showing now, as if sleep brought him neither comfort nor escape. She made a small movement as if to reach over and touch him and then checked it. The cushion fell from behind her and she realized that he must have put it there. The small act of kindness was suddenly unbearable and she buried her face in the cushion fighting back the tears.

FOUR

Two days later, in the early hours before dawn broke, a man in a brown Volvo drove out of his small Georgian mansion on the outskirts of London. Traffic was light and he reached the cottage at twenty minutes to five. He wondered if three days of incarceration with the Berringer woman would fan old flames of ardour or turn Mackilroy off. The latter would be the more expedient reaction and he thought it the more likely. At the commencement of the kidnapping he had told Mackilroy that the girl wouldn't be hurt. Mackilroy had appeared to believe him. Mackilroy, however, wasn't a fool. It was a case of balancing the degree of his involvement with the cause against the depth of any existing feeling he might have for a love affair gone stale. The slight risk that his loyalty might be on the wrong side had to be taken.

The man parked the car by the barn and then went into it. What he had to do soiled his well kept fingers and he made a moue of distaste as he got on with it. Several minutes later he entered the cottage with his own key. Mack had heard the car and was walking through into the living room as the man came in.

The man noticed that he came from his own bedroom and that he had been alone in it. He was either playing it very slowly or the rot had started.

Mack said, 'Well?' And then he noticed what the man was carrying. 'Christ – no!'

'Not an aesthetic method, I grant you, but not painful either, I promised you she wouldn't be hurt. Get your cassette recorder.'

Mack struggled with revulsion. 'You can't do that to her!'

'Damn it, man, hurry. It has to happen in her bedroom and now before she's fully awake.'

He waited until the cassette was on the table and switched on and then he gently toed open Dee's bedroom door. Vaguely aware of voices and yet associating them with her dream she awoke slowly. The skittering noise on the floorboards brought her more fully awake. The rat, released from its box, was exploring its new terrain and finding no exit began to panic. Its leap on the bed was made with no lethal intent and its long lean body landed on Dee's hand. Her screams froze it into immobility and it remained heavy and warm and obscene on her flesh for several seconds before she flung it off. Mack cornered it by the wardrobe and killed it with his shoe and then he held her until her scream became tears. He rocked her backwards and forwards like a child. 'Hush now – it's gone. It didn't hurt you.' And then oddly, 'Dee, I'm sorry. Darling, I'm sorry.' She leaned her head against him weeping. 'My hand – oh, God, my hand. Oh, Mack, take me away. I can't bear it. I can't bear it.'

The man in the living room, thoroughly satisfied, pocketed the cassette and went back to his car. With a little doctoring the tape should suit his purpose excellently. He put the Volvo into neutral and let it slide quietly down the track towards the road. The Berringer woman hadn't heard him come, it would be just as well if she didn't hear him go. It had been stupid of Mackilroy to comfort her with words, but it had probably been a gut reaction he couldn't help. Mackilroy's sympathy could well prove to be a nuisance. If it were, he would have to be taken off the assignment and the girl would have to be guarded by someone else.

He parked the car at a convenient lay-by and wiped Mackilroy's words off. The silence between her screams and her plea to be taken away was convincingly ominous.

And now for Berringer himself.

He reached the Kensington flat at breakfast time, parked the car neatly in a convenient space almost opposite the front door, and ran nimbly up the steps. The strict discipline of years at sea hadn't been eroded by five years of sedentary work at the Admiralty and at fifty-seven he was still as physically fit as he had ever been.

Briony answered the door. He noticed that she still wore the tank top and brown slacks she had worn on the night of the bombing. He had observed the operation from the car park and been annoyed with her for not dressing more suitably. Her casual get-up had been conspicuous. This morning she had added a blue lambswool jacket. He saw it as a compromise and it tallied with what he knew of Berringer. The jacket, obviously his wife's, was lent to keep the girl warm, but she hadn't the run of the wardrobe. She greeted him briefly and then stood aside, stony-faced, as he stepped into the hall. Once again he congratulated himself on the fact that it was on his personal recommendation that she was given the assignment. There would be no emotional involvement here.

'Where's Berringer?'

'In the bathroom.'

'How is it going?'

'As planned.'

'Any difficulties?'

'No – it's just as you said it would be.' She was lying quite calmly. The difficulties were, she knew, of her own creating. She was supposed to get under David's skin like an insistent and annoying mosquito and still retain her cool. That he should get under hers was a weakness she had no intention of admitting to.

She showed him into the sitting-room and went and tapped on the bathroom door. 'There's someone to see you.'

After three days of mounting tension David's nerves were nearer snapping point than she realized. He finished shaving, but his hand wasn't as steady as it had been before and he was too liberal with the after-shave lotion. He swore and rubbed his face with the towel. It didn't do to greet a mobster smelling like a Persian Garden, but the bloody stuff wouldn't come off. He grinned sourly at his reflection. So this was it. The big moment.

He went along the corridor to the sitting-room and then on the threshold he halted in astonishment. Standing by the green marble fireplace and casually lighting a cheroot was a man he had known for years.

'Admiral Jackson!'

'Good morning, Berringer. I'm sorry to walk in on you at this most inconvenient hour of the morning. Have you breakfasted?'

The steel that had replaced David's skeleton once again became bone. He relaxed, relief mingling with disappointment. So it wasn't the big moment, after all, the waiting would go on.

'Yes, I've breakfasted, but you'll join me in coffee? Sit down, Admiral, it's good to see you.'

The Admiral's visit, for whatever reason, seemed heaven-sent. If he could keep Briony out of the room for long enough he would be able to outline the situation to him. Jackson's cool, analytical mind would come up with the right advice and he could start taking action.

He called out to Briony to percolate some fresh coffee. 'Give it about fifteen minutes.'

She came to the kitchen door and nodded without a word. Prepared for an argument, an insistence that she should remain in the room with them, her acquiescence took him by surprise.

He closed the sitting-room door. 'I've something urgent to say to you.'

Jackson's white hair, silvered by a ray of morning sunlight, looked like a nimbus. His dark eyes smiled quizzically, 'I know.' He tapped the ash from his cheroot into a green onyx ashtray.

David felt a lifting of the spirits. 'You know! You mean I've been sweating here for the last three days wondering how the hell to get help and the police have been working on it all the time?'

'Well – no – I'm afraid I didn't mean that.'

'Then what do you mean? If not the police, then who? How does your department come into it?'

'The Admiralty? Only in a small way, I'm afraid, but hopefully large enough to be effective.'

David said flatly. 'I don't understand you. I doubt whether you understand me. After the bomb in the Silver Swan restaurant, my wife was abducted. The girl who planted the bomb is here with me now. My wife is being held hostage. I am to be visited by someone who will give me the terms on which she will be released.'

'Yes,' the Admiral repeated it, 'I know.'

David sat down. His mind felt as if it housed a hive of bees. 'If you know, then I'm sure you have a perfectly reasonable explanation. Tell me, I want to know, too.'

The Admiral's smile showed genuine amusement. 'All right – calm yourself.' The girl had obviously done her work well. Berringer's fatigue showed mostly in his voice. He wondered how much sleep he had had since Briony had started mounting guard.

He suggested that as the explanation was likely to take some time it would be as well to have the coffee brought in immediately. 'Tell Briony to bring in a cup for herself.'

Even more deeply mystified David said, 'You know her?'

'Yes, since she was a child. My wife and I were of some help to her when her parents died. Her father was killed. Did she tell you?'

'Yes, a car accident. But I don't see what all this has to do with the present situation.'

'Not very much, perhaps. It was a hit and run – the driver was never caught.'

'I still don't see.'

'No, how could you?' The Admiral stood up. 'May I presume to hurry her – or will you?'

51

David made a helpless gesture and then went over to the door and called out to Briony. 'Bring the coffee now – and three cups.'

Her voice came back sharply. 'I'm not a blasted maid.'

Jackson bit back a smile. She was behaving in character. Tough, intelligent, charmless.

She brought in the coffee and poured it for the three of them. Why the Admiral should try to make a social occasion of it was beyond her. Why didn't he give it out straight and blunt and have done? She took her own cup to the window and pulled the chair around so that the sun was behind her. Not sure of her own reactions it seemed wiser to keep her face in shadow. David, about twenty years the Admiral's junior, looked like a seaman trying to steer through fog with no radar to help him. She wondered how he would shape up to the facts when he got them.

Jackson sipped the coffee, decided it was appalling, and put the cup down. David, who hadn't touched his, was sitting back in his chair, his arms folded.

Jackson chose his lead-in carefully. 'What I have to say to you will probably shock you – at first. It may seem senseless. It may seem criminal. Before you throw it out I want you to consider it with extreme care. I think, perhaps, before I start, I would like you to tell me your opinion of me. I know that could be an embarrassing question. Be as rude as you like.' The smile came and went.

It was an embarrassing question. Genuine liking – even admiration – tended to cloy when put into words. David said brusquely. 'You had a distinguished career at sea – is that what you want me to say?'

'I want you to say what you feel you must say.'

'You were offered a knighthood and declined it – is that relevant?'

'No – but go on.'

'In testimonial language you are held by everyone in high regard. Intelligent – high principled.' He flushed with mounting

52

anger. 'Damn it – is that what you came for – an eulogy?'

'No – and be patient, David. None of this is easy. Would you say I was the type of person to uphold law and order?'

'Yes.' He added, 'That would go without saying.'

'Quite. I hoped you would agree. Now how would you define law and order?'

'Reasonable behaviour, I suppose, and humane laws to enforce reasonable behaviour.'

'The ability to walk the streets at night without fear of mugging. The ability to dine at – shall we say The Silver Swan – without loss of limb – or sight – or even life. The freedom to choose one's creed whatever that creed might be. Would you consider that way of life to be reasonable?'

'Naturally.'

'And would you say that we're living that type of life now?'

'In view of present events – no.'

'So where would you place the blame?'

'It's hard to say. As we're talking about order I suppose your question throws the emphasis onto law. Our police do their best under difficult circumstances. I fail to see how they could be improved. And I fail to see where this conversation is getting us. If there is a point then I'd be glad if you'd come to it.'

'I am coming to it, but it can't be rushed. We had got as far as law enforcement. We both know that the armed wing of the police force and the helicopter units are effective only up to a point. They're outnumbered – just as the Anti-Terrorist Unit is out-witted. A big problem requires a big solution.'

'Meaning a monolithic police force?' An academic argument that more properly concerned the Home Office seemed to David aggravatingly incongruous in its present context, but he tried to answer reasonably. 'It wouldn't be possible. Even if it were, it wouldn't be desirable. What is your argument trying to justify – a police state? Fascism? What?'

The Admiral smoked in silence for a moment or two. 'You're using emotive words emotively.' He handed over his cheroot case. 'I'm sorry – do you smoke these?'

David declined. 'Go on.'

'No, David, I want you to go on. I'm not handing ideas to you. I want you to think and come up with your own. Let's put the various isms on one side. Would you say the sickness was in the people?'

'It seems that way – yes.'

'And how far would you say the sickness has spread – to the so called silent majority, for instance?'

'No. No, I've never believed that.'

'Then why the hell don't they get up and shout – through apathy – through fear – through what . . .?'

'Through lack of the right leadership – is that what you're getting at?'

'Is that what you think?'

'If it were it would throw the onus on . . .', he hesitated and the Admiral said it for him, 'on you.'

'Yes – and on others like me. We represent the people.' He followed the argument through. 'And so you place the blame at the top – at leadership level?'

'Wouldn't you agree?'

'I suppose so. Are you trying to say that democracy has failed?'

'Look around you and answer that for yourself.'

'But the rot is world wide. Every nation has its problems.' He made an impatient movement. 'If you're not pleading Fascism, then what? Frankly I don't understand you.'

'Then let's reduce it to the simplest terms. Ideally a democratic system should work – but the conditions now are not ideal. There's a substratum of terrorism and it's growing. Three party bickering is about as effective as a Maori war dance in the face of inter-planetary missiles. What's needed at the top is strength and unity – not division. A coalition of the best brains in every sphere of government. A Group of dedicated well-chosen forceful leaders with a common cause.' He noticed David's expression. 'I see you've already heard of us as the Group. A pity. You've had time to form a prejudice.' There was condemnation in the look he gave Briony. She looked away.

'Yes, I've heard of you that way – but go on.'

'As I was saying – a coalition of the best brains with no party axe to grind. A Group working together very strongly for the common good.'

'An idealized concept.'

'On the contrary. If nothing is done now – what happens? A steady and continuing erosion.'

'Coalition governments have been tried before.'

'Granted, but we're not speaking of the same thing. Take the electoral system . . . it's like a game of chance. Party representatives present themselves, some good, some bad, the majority indifferent. How do the people know what they're getting – a baby-kisser with a mind like a moron – or a man with real leadership ability?'

'You mean we should kill off the electoral system, feed details of candidates into a computer and abide by the result?'

'Yes – more or less. Excellence. Aptitude. Special gifts in special spheres. The right man in the right place at the right time.'

'Utopian rubbish!'

'Not at all. You're talking off the top of your head. You haven't had time to think it out yet.'

'As a philosophy it's attractive – but it can't be anything more than pie in the sky.'

'Oh yes, it can – and it is.'

The Admiral leaned forward in his chair. 'For over two years now we have been collecting our team – all right – our Group – I won't shirk the word. We've infiltrated committed men with very special qualities into the workforce of the nation. They're there waiting to take over when the time is right. We have Civil Servants at all levels. There is no Ministry, including yours, that hasn't been infiltrated. We have men in key positions in the media. Newspaper owners. Journalists. We have business men – scientists – engineers – teachers. And men on the shop floor who have enough guts and presence and intelligence to shout back at the bosses – either union boss – or owner boss – and make themselves heard and carry the people with them.'

He looked keenly at David. 'And now you're listening, aren't you? Come on, bombard me with arguments. That's what I want.'

Incredulity was the only rational reaction. 'Do you seriously expect me to believe in a nebulous army of supermen who are ready to take over the British Isles at the drop of a hat – or a blast on a trumpet? For God's sake it sounds the most marvellous piece of rubbish I've ever heard. How are you going to oust the present lot and replace them with your wonderful crew, always presupposing they exist?'

'They exist all right. I could give you name and rank number of each and everyone. A lot of the names you know already – and would surprise you. But most you've never heard of – but you will. And how do we oust the others? That's not as difficult as you think. They will be ousted by the people themselves when they're so sickened by the present state of affairs that they are prepared to turn around and do something about it. And when that happens we will be there. They need us. They want us. They're sick now and they're frightened now. When they're a lot sicker and a lot more frightened they'll call a halt and an about face. They'll shout for leadership. Inspired, intelligent leadership and we'll give it to them.'

'But first a blood bath – is that it? I think I'm beginning to understand you.'

'I think you are. We're dealing with a plague as great as any of the great plagues of the past – and how were they cured? By controlled injections of the very bugs that started them off. Oh yes, we bombed the Silver Swan restaurant and some of the other bomb

56

outrages were ours, too. I use the word outrage advisedly. They are
outrages. They're abominations. And they're going to come thicker
and faster until the public throws off its lethargy and screams for an
end to it.'

Even an insane argument could sound plausible, David thought,
when the brain cells were too fatigued to combat it. 'And why have
you come here this morning to say all this to me?'

'Because of all the better known Parliamentarians you're the one
with the special quality of leadership we need.'

There was a short silence while he let his words sink in. 'And
now I'll tell you how you'll react. Astonishment – yes, obviously.
Amused disbelief – again that's obvious. You're not a bighead. You
have the right degree of modesty. Not too little. Not too much. And
it's natural to you. It's not assumed. You can be manipulated if you
respect the manipulator. When I state that fact it doesn't make you
angry, because you are intelligent and you know it is true. You have
an aura of integrity. The people trust you. You're honest with them
and they respect your honesty. You speak well – to them and not at
them. You forget the sound of your own voice because what you say
matters to you – and to them. You're young, but not too young.
They've had their fill of father figures – old men with old ideas . . .
And shall I tell you what you're thinking now? The idea of power
has come into your mind and you're rejecting it. You've never
wanted absolute power and you're not being offered it. We want a
front man, not a dictator. You'll be the mouthpiece of brilliant
minds who'll work in concert for the common good.'

'I will be this – I will do that . . . Quite honestly, Jackson, I think
you're more than a little mad.'

'No, you don't. You're giving me a conventional response. The
idea is not only feasible – it's attractive. You'll deny it, of course.
It's too soon for you to do anything else. But you'll start turning it
over in your mind – you'll start picking at it – you'll search for loose
ends. You'll push it away from you. You'll say it's impossible. And

then you won't be so sure. Try to find the loose ends now and let me see if I can tie them for you. Come on, demonstrate the impossibility of it, I'm listening.'

David turned to Briony. 'You knew about this?'

She hadn't spoken for a long time and made a small nervous jerk of surprise at being addressed. 'Yes.'

'And what so-called special qualities have you?'

'Don't pick on me as your opponent, David. Put your questions to the Admiral.'

'All right – then the Admiral can answer for you.'

'Intelligence and commitment and a deep abhorrence of violence.' Jackson's answer was smooth.

'What? You got her to plant a bomb and you can say that?'

'I can, indeed. The bomb wasn't intended to kill. It was mistimed.'

'I don't believe you. You're escalating violence in order to push the public into such a pitch of loathing for violence that they'll become malleable to any new regime that seems to offer them order. Can you seriously tell me that the timing wasn't deliberately delayed?'

Jackson, aware that the girl was looking at him with deep anxiety, gave her the necessary lie. 'In this particular instance the bomb wasn't intended to kill.' He turned the conversation away from her. 'We don't like the means we have to use, but the end is worth everything. We didn't create the violence in the first place. The sickness isn't in us.'

'And is there a time-limit to the escalation? For how many years do you stoke the flames until the whole damn place goes up?'

'Years? Think again, David, and get your timing right. You know the situation better than most.'

David was silent for several minutes. He felt punch drunk and battered. He abandoned argument for fact. 'And Dee? Where and why are you holding Dee?'

'Somewhere safe. I know our methods are bizarre. If it's any

58

consolation to you, we've never had to force anyone before. We're forcing you because we can't get anyone to measure up to you that the people will accept. We believe that when you've had time to give it thought – when you can see the full mechanism of it – how smoothly it's running – how advanced our planning already is – you'll become as committed as any of us. In these early days, if we don't hold Dee, your scepticism won't allow you a fair analysis. You need time. You're getting it.'

'Under duress.'

'Yes, under duress.'

'And if I still insist that I can't go along with it – that I can't believe in it – that I'll take what you've told me to official quarters to deal with – then what?'

'Then your wife won't come back to you.'

It came out staccato sharp. 'You mean you'd kill her?'

The answer was equally sharp. 'Yes.'

Briony made a sudden movement and her coffee cup spilt its contents on the cream Wilton carpet.

Neither man looked at her.

A pulse was drumming in David's head. It throbbed and hummed as it sent the accelerated blood flow through his arteries.

Jackson watched his reaction as if he were a specimen on a slide. He was behaving the way Carling, one of the leading psychiatrists in the country, had told him he would behave. Shock. Total rejection. Adjustment – but nor for some time. He had been told to start with reasoned argument – to present the case – and then to apply shock tactics.

He applied them. 'We need you and we intend having you. I'm sorry to have to do this, but you need convincing that we're serious.' He took the cassette out of his pocket and gave it to Briony. 'You know how these things work. Play it when I've gone.'

He was a realist and saw no point in courting physical injury. Berringer wouldn't hurt the girl.

He stood up and went over to the door. 'When you've heard what is on the cassette consider yourself free to go about your Parliamentary duties again. We'll be keeping tabs on you, but not obviously. Everything you do will be reported back to us. Make some plausible excuse to your friends about your wife's absence. Briony will stay on here until she returns. There's no reason in the world why she shouldn't return eventually. It's up to you.'

'Wait. You can't walk out now. There's more to be said.' David put a hand out to stop him.

'There'll be plenty to be said later. Hear what's on the cassette first.'

The Admiral shook off his restraining hand and then as if taking his leave after a perfectly normal social occasion gave them both a brief smile before going down the corridor to the hall door.

Briony waited until she heard it close behind him.

David, unaware of the nature of the tape, expected to hear more ravings along the same lines and took hardly any notice as Briony put the cassette on the table. She pressed the button and the tape ran silently for two or three minutes. Fearing that she had done something wrong she was about to press it again when Dee's screams tore through the room. Then came the terrible silence, followed by the sound of weeping and 'My hand – oh, God, my hand. Oh, Mack, take me away. I can't bear it! I can't bear it!'

David in a convulsive movement drove his fist into the cassette and then drove it again and again until his knuckles bled. He had a primitive urge to kill. To destroy the room around him. Fury and horror gripped him so that the room seemed a red haze. Her pain burned inside him so that his body was aflame with her pain. He would do anything to give her ease – to get her back. They had baited his trap with care. He would have to do everything they demanded he should do. He would have to get her out of there and at any cost.

He watched as Briony gathered up the shattered cassette. There was blood on her fingers. His blood. She looked sick and frightened like a spectator at an execution.

FIVE

Mack said, 'I've a television in the van. Hold the door open for me while I carry it in.'

He hadn't been ordered to get the set. It was something he was doing of his own volition. Dee's moods since the episode with the rat weren't easy to take. Her first reaction was to allow him a closer physical intimacy than they had had for some time and then at the last moment she had pushed him away. That she had wanted to cling to him for comfort was something he understood, but he hadn't the kind of temperament that would enable him to give comfort sexlessly. She should have known him well enough to know that and her rejection irked him. The following long period of silence during which she had sat on the chair by the window and looked out at the endless fields had got on his nerves. He had padded around the kitchen making meals for them, meals she had scarcely bothered to eat. Eventually, after whistling the dog over from the barn he had told her he was going out.

She had shown some interest. 'Am I allowed to go with you?'

'Sorry, Dee, no.'

Her acceptance of the fact was almost lethargic. 'All right. Have it your way, but tell your blasted dog to sit outside. I'm not having it in.'

Now as he came in with the set she looked at it with amused

contempt. 'So I'm to be allowed home comforts, am I? Why didn't you bring books?'

'You can have books, too, if you want them.' He put the television on a small corner table and began fixing the plug. It was a portable set with its own aerial.

'Next time I'll give you a list.'

'Of books?'

'Books – a new carpet – curtains – furniture – everything to make a home from home.'

He was busy with the screwdriver. 'Don't be so petulant. You're becoming a bore.'

'If I'm becoming a bore, it's because I'm bored. I've been frightened – disgusted – and now I'm bored. I never thought that being here alone with you would make me feel so – so—' she gestured – 'well – nothing – like a hole.'

They both, despite their annoyance, grinned faintly at the ineptness of the word.

'When will David come for me, do you think?'

He gave it to her straight. 'Not for sometime. That's why you have to sit it out here as patiently as you can.'

'But for God's sake what has he been told to do – and why isn't he doing it?'

'He will do it – and you'll find out what it is eventually.'

She felt like screaming at him. It was the answer he kept parroting at her.

'In the meantime,' he said, 'look at the box. After all, it entertains some of the people most of the time. Now's your chance to get hooked.'

In an effort to accept the inevitable, she tried to make the best of things. Towards the end of the first week she had sufficiently come to terms with the situation to start playing a small part in the running of the cottage. Mack bought the food and she cooked it. They both washed up. He bought rat killer at her insistence and she sprinkled it in all the rooms. On fine days they walked in the fields, but they walked for the most part without talking. On wet days they played cards or watched the television. At night they went to their separate rooms. The relationship between them was like a quiet fire smouldering. It would either blaze or die. She thought it already dead, but he wasn't so sure.

The news programmes became a regular habit. They watched every one. She still hoped to hear the announcement 'Mysterious disappearance of MP's wife.' It would imply that something was being done. The total silence seemed to deny her her very identity. What were her friends thinking? Had the hospital rung to find out why she hadn't been around with the library trolley? She had promised to meet David's sister for a shopping spree. She couldn't remember the date, but it must be about now. Had Sally rung up to find out if it was still on? If David had answered the phone, what had he said? Would anybody ever do anything? Was she fated to sit here in this squalid place with Mack for the rest of her days?

She felt a cool draught as he opened the outer door and came in from the barn. She guessed there was some means of communication there. A telephone? A transmitter? He wouldn't allow her in. Not that she wanted to go. The dog was there and the rats were there. She wished each would feast upon the other.

Mack said, 'News time,' and switched on the set. There was an undercurrent of excitement in the voice.

The announcer's voice echoed it. 'Less than twenty minutes ago, a bomb exploded in the National Gallery. It's not yet known how many casualties there are. The damage is extensive and several priceless paintings have been destroyed.' The cameras, unable to get close to the portico of the Gallery, ranged up and down the street as the police cleared the area and firemen moved in with their pumps. A reporter in the street took up the story. 'There's a fire, but it seems to be contained. Had the bomb exploded half an hour later, after closing time, the Gallery would have been empty. It's thought some people were trampled in the rush for the exit.' He pushed his way through the crowds with his microphone and reached a man who was being given first aid by a St John Ambulance man. 'Are you badly hurt, sir?' The man, too dazed to answer, shook his head. Another man beside him shouted furiously. 'It's a bloody outrage! How long do we have to stand for this? Some of the most beautiful pictures in the world were in there. What's going to be done about it – that's what I want to know? Is everything worth while going to be destroyed while we just stand back and watch?' A woman in a headscarf chipped in. 'Never mind the pictures. What about the people? There were kids in that lot. A party from a school. I saw them go in. Sod your pictures. We can do without them – what about the kids?' An older man, bald, bearded and quietly spoken, took it up. 'I agree – people before pictures. But it's monstrous that we should lose our heritage of art. When is this anarchy going to be stopped? When are we going to find our strength again and start hitting back. What are the leaders doing? Damn all. We have no leaders. Our country is being run like a primary school by a staff of elderly incompetents. Sack them, I say. Get some new blood in, I say. Let Britain show she still has guts and brains and can cope with this sort of thing and stop it.' There was a growling murmur of assent and then the picture switched back to the studio. The announcer said, 'Feelings are running high, as you saw. We will continue to keep you informed and there will be a longer bulletin at nine o'clock.'

Dee said, 'Well, at least I can't blame you for that. Unless you exploded it by remote control when you were feeding the dog.' She was shocked, but not as shocked as she would have been if she hadn't been involved in the Silver Swam bombing. That was personal. This wasn't.

Mack switched off the set. The rest of the news wasn't relevant. Sam Davidson, the reporter on the spot, had got an excellent reaction. It sounded genuine. It might well have been. The majority

66

of people felt that way only the majority weren't usually good at expressing it.

Dee was looking at him closely. 'Mack – did you know this was going to happen?'

'How could I possibly know?'

'That's not a denial.'

'All right – then – no.'

She didn't know if he lied or not. 'Doesn't it bother you that it has happened?'

'Of course it bothers me. Do you suppose I'm indifferent to loss of life – to the destruction of beauty?'

It sounded trite in the present context and she spoke with a degree of bitterness. 'Do you remember that day we arranged to meet by the Portrait of Mrs Siddons? You were late and it was raining. It was our first meeting after Scotland. I thought you weren't coming.'

'Yes, I remember.' He reached over to touch her, but she drew away.

They put the news on again at nine o'clock. The death toll was eighteen. The Hogarth collection was totally destroyed. An art critic spoke briefly about Hogarth. The outside cameras zoomed in on the casualty department of the nearby hospital. A harassed looking doctor was asked how things were and he said bloody and he hadn't time to talk. The newscaster said that a special programme would follow the news. Instead of the scheduled play, a member of the public who was at the disaster at the time, a Mr Reginald Drayton, would give his views to the MP of his Constituency, Mr David Berringer, presently the Minister of Defence.

Dee said 'David!' Astonishment followed by delight transformed her so that for the first time for days she felt she had come fully alive. He was going to talk on the box. She was actually going to see and hear him. 'Mack, David's coming on!'

'Yes.' Mack silently congratulated whoever was responsible at the BBC for arranging the interview so quickly. The general presentation had been chaotic up to now. The sandwiching of the Hogarth man right in the middle of the medical information hadn't been brilliant.

Dee, impatient with the rest of the news, couldn't sit still and began pacing up and down and saying under her breath, 'Oh, come on – come on – come *on*!'

The presenter was a comparative newcomer who was beginning to make a name for himself, Leo Carradine. He had authority without acid. He handled the discussion with tact and control, selecting the questions carefully, manipulating without appearing to do so. David, the only amateur, felt as if he were being carefully balanced somewhere above ground by two experienced trapeze artists. And then he began to get the hang of it. He congratulated Drayton for being in the area and managing to escape injury. Drayton gave a graphic description of the people he had seen hurt. Carradine listed the number of bombing incidents during the last few months and asked David if he thought the growing violence could ever be contained and if so how? David replied that it depended on the people as a whole. It was up to the people. It was up to men like Drayton, law-abiding, hard-working men, who wanted a peaceful stable existence for themselves and their families, to stop being so complacent. To which Drayton said that the people were powerless on their own. They need leadership, the right leadership, now. Carradine asked if Drayton could define the right leadership. He had a Minister of the Crown sitting beside him, the representative of his Constituency. Was he criticizing Berringer's leadership? Drayton said that if only more men like Berringer could be given greater authority, then the ship of state might weather the storm and reach the sort of harbour everyone wanted. David thanked him for the confidence he placed in him. He had always, he said, tried to serve the people with the whole of his strength and enthusiasm and with integrity. It appalled him that mindless violence was growing out of control like a malignant tumour and as yet no appropriate action had been taken to halt it. Carradine asked if the canker in the nation should be excised by the knife – in other words should violence be countered with violence? To which David replied that violence and all forms of criminality should be countered by a strong, united government, backed by a show of military strength as and when necessary. Up to now we had side-stepped our problems. The subversives of all clans, colour, and creed continued to erode the strength of the country and the politicians continued to turn a blind eye – or to bray ineffectively – or even in some cases condone. It wasn't good enough. It wasn't leadership. It was a backing out of responsibility. We were being harassed on all sides and we would continue to be harassed on all sides until the British people decided to make a determined effort to stop the harassment. He turned to Drayton. 'You say the people are ineffective on their own. Not true. You, the people, make the leaders of the country. You get the leaders you deserve. You and the Government are a corporate body – Parliament is your mouthpiece and your right hand.'

Drayton said, 'If thy right hand offend thee, cut it off.'

Carradine quickly interposed with a smiling, 'but preferably get a competent surgeon to do it. In case the viewers don't quiet get the point there – how would you define the right hand?'

David, momentarily startled, regained his composure. 'The status quo. We can't go along much longer as we are. To survive we must be ready for change. We are battered and bloody and right on our knees. We must stand up and do something about it. We're not a land of morons, or defeatists, or flabby yes-men. We've been pushed around enough. At some stage soon we shall cry halt. At some stage soon we shall rally the people into positive, dramatic, and purposeful action. The power is in the hands of that part of the British public which is cognizant of the perils of the present time and has the intelligence and the courage to take strong and decisive action under the control of strong and decisive leadership.'

'But if the strong and decisive leadership doesn't exist?' Drayton's question was thrust in quickly.

'It can be made to. It will be made to. It has to be made to.'

At that point the programme was faded out.

Dee, utterly astonished, said weakly, 'But good God . . .' and couldn't express her sentiments any further. This was a David she had never seen before – a rabble raiser or a crusader – certainly not the moderate man she had married. The fact that the programme hadn't been allowed to run its full length occurred to her 'They stopped him!'

'Yes, but not in time. He was magnificent.' Mack's praise was genuine. Berringer had taken the part upon himself like a pro. He had never been able to understand why Berringer was chosen for the rôle. Now he knew.

Dee said, 'The PM will give him a rocket. He might even be kicked out.'

'A rocket – yes. Kicked out – no. At least not for a while – and then it will be too late.'

'Too late—? What are you talking about?'

He wished he could tell her the full story but allowed himself only, 'He's made a good impression – it will be a lasting one – any move later can only be a move up.'

'I didn't realize you liked him.'

'Neither did I,' Mack said, 'until now.'

Dee had noticed the lines of strain in David's face. Despite the firmness, the confidence, of his extraordinary performance, she sensed that it hadn't come easily to him. The possibility that he had done it under duress occurred to her.

'Was his performance tonight anything to do with the terms of my release?'

His hesitation before answering confirmed the affirmative. 'Don't press me, Dee. I can't give you any details yet. I will when I can.'

70

'Is that other woman still with him?'

'Briony? I don't know. It seems he's free to carry on as normal, so probably not.'

He detected relief in her expression and knew he had told her what she wanted to be told. Briony, and the possible threat of Briony, was something she could understand.

She went over the old ground again in her mind, but couldn't find anything relevant to the present time. Certainly nothing relevant to David or to her. She caught a glimpse of herself in the mirror over the fireplace. Her face showed as much strain as David's. Her hair was lank. She was becoming a hag. Tired, frustrated, worried, and angered by a situation that didn't begin to make sense, she told Mack abruptly that she was going to wash her hair.

Her reaction, wholly feminine, amused him. 'It's late. How are you going to dry it?'

'By that wretched little fire, I suppose, put some wood on it.'

She washed her hair with perfumed toilet soap and rinsed it clumsily wetting her sweater. She took the sweater off and put a towel around her shoulders. When she returned to the living room the fire was blazing up and she crouched beside it.

'I'll rub it for you.' He took the towel from her and rubbed briskly. And then he let the towel drop and his fingers moved gently through her hair and massaged the nape of her neck.

The response was there. He kept massaging gently. 'Dee?'

Her voice came hoarsely. 'No.'

She got up onto her knees and pulled the towel away from him. Her face was pink in the firelight, her eyes refused to look at him. 'But why?'

'Because I don't choose to be here. Because you won't let me go. It's the only freedom I've got.'

The considered answer surprised him. She wanted him physically as much as he wanted her. 'And so you'll withhold yourself like a

71

bloody vestal virgin – out of spite?'

'I shall withhold myself like a married woman with a husband I happen to love.'

'Crap.' He was angry.

'It's true.'

'It's taken you a hell of a long time to find out.'

'Yes,' she said, 'it has.' She leaned forward to the flames and let her hair fall like a curtain before her eyes.

He couldn't see her expression and derived some comfort from the fact that she found it impossible to say whilst looking directly at him.

Briony, too, had watched the broadcast with considerable interest. As far as she could tell, it couldn't be faulted. He had gone nervously, but his nerves hadn't been evident. The visit of his sister shortly before he had to leave for Broadcasting House hadn't helped. She had taken Briony for an au-pair. Apparently Dee's only household help were au-pairs who came and went at irregular intervals. According to David, Dee liked to practise her French and German on them. The sister was called Sally. She was short, plump and suspicious. She had arranged to have an outing with Dee and she wanted to know where Dee was. Briony, who was asked it first, said Scotland. It was an obvious association and it had tripped off her tongue without thought. David, who hadn't overheard, said Birmingham – visiting an old school friend. His sister had asked with scant tact which of them was lying and David in a burst of annoyance had told her not to talk like a fool. She had left shortly afterwards in an aura of ice.

The difficulty of sharing the flat with him when he quite obviously wanted to be left on his own was making Briony's nerves as taut as his. The sound of Dee's screams on the cassette had shocked her deeply. Guilt by association, if not by deed, weighed on her. She wanted to comfort him, but didn't know how. Her suggestion that she should iron a clean shirt for him before he left for the BBC was about the best she could do. He declined crisply. He had, he said, several shirts and all ironed. 'Then don't wear that tie. It doesn't match your suit.'

'If you must be around, Briony, then please leave me alone.'

'I'm only trying to help.'

'Well – don't. I've enough on my mind without bothering about trivia. Is the presenter of the programme tonight one of your people?'

'Yes.'

'Thank God for that – what will he do, pass me notes?' It was sarcastic.

'If you needed to have notes passed to you, you wouldn't be asked to do the broadcast at all. You'll cope and you'll cope very well.'

He would, he thought, dance the dance of a hanged man. With luck he'd get all the contortions right.

When he returned later that night he was physically and emotionally exhausted. Briony had a meal waiting for him. She wasn't a good cook but she had done her best to produce a fairly edible casserole. He told her he had already eaten in the BBC canteen.

'What – sandwiches?'

'Yes.'

'You can't exist on sandwiches. Try some of this.'

'I'm not hungry.'

'David, you've got to survive.'

He knew that. He had to eat, sleep and be fit, if not for his own sake then for Dee's. He drew his chair up to the table and ate without enthusiasm.

She told him at last that she had seen the performance and that he was very good. He wondered why she hadn't said so before. She was an odd creature, he thought. Sometimes she chose her words with great care so that they pierced like a matador's barbs. At other

73

times her sensitivity surprised him.

'You took your time to come out with it.'

'I didn't think you wanted to be reminded.'

'I don't.'

It occurred to him that as she knew Carradine was one of the Group she might be able to give him the names of some of the others, but she declined to be drawn. 'They'll make themselves known to you as time goes on.'

He asked bitterly, 'How? A two-fingered handshake – a scout's salute – or a well-aimed spit in the eye?'

She sighed. 'You've got to take us seriously.'

'What the hell did you think I was doing tonight?' So seriously, he thought, that I half believed it.

The next morning he was carpeted by the Prime Minister. He expected it and didn't attempt any defence. What the PM said was valid criticism and he agreed with every word of it. 'Luckily,' the PM said, 'the Press has played it down with the exception of *The Galaxy*. They've given it the full treatment. Have you seen it?' He pushed a copy of the paper across the desk. David looked at a picture of himself taken a few years back for the election campaign, the one that Dee had teased him about. 'The good old British bulldog image,' she had said, 'but handsome with it. If that doesn't inspire confidence in the voters then nothing will.' The write-up in the *Galaxy*'s leader column was along the same lines. The adjectives solid, thoughtful, courageous were used. A man of our time, it said. 'A man with the perspicacity to assess the true seriousness of the situation and place the blame fairly where it belongs – with the weak leadership of the country. And it's no Party matter. The crack in the fabric cuts right through the whole edifice of government and the crack is widening. It takes men of Berringer's calibre to see the danger and to warn us of it. He has put truth before Party politics and could well have endangered his own career by so doing.'

The Prime Minister said dryly, 'The last sentence, of course, ensures that I shall do nothing other than tell you what a Godalmighty fool you've made of yourself and to warn you not to do anything so dangerously undermining again.' He added. 'The paper is owned by Russ Trevelyan. He was in the Honours List this January. An OBE.' It was bitter. 'He's not known to you by any chance?'

'No.'

'Well, I'll take your word for that. You, quite obviously, are known to him.'

His anger a little abated, he walked with David to the door. 'If you need leave, take it. You don't look well. Don't press yourself too hard.'

'Thank you, Prime Minister, but I don't need leave – I'm perfectly fit.'

'I always thought you were – no-one more so.' It was quite evident that the Prime Minister was referring to the state of his mind.

The business in the House was finished by six forty-five. Only half aware of what had been going on, David forgot it completely as he walked along Westminster Bridge. The distant siren of a ship on the Thames had the mournful sound of a requiem. The Spring sky, sulphur yellow and banked with clouds, threatened coming rain. His anxiety for Dee was with him constantly. The memory of her screams was like an ever present tinnitus that his ears couldn't shut out. Her plea on the cassette had been for Mackilroy to take her away. It implied that whatever was happening to her, Mackilroy wasn't the perpetrator. The on-looker, then? But God damn him, how could he just stand there and watch? He kept dreaming of torture. The cells of his brain produced sleep-scenes of tortures so horrific that he awoke sweating and moaning and fearful of sleeping again.

He felt emasculated by inactivity. The need to get up and do something to help her and his inability to do anything other than what he was told sapped his confidence and made him ashamed of his impotence. If she were not involved he would have contacted the Special Branch and at any cost to himself he would have helped them to move in on the Group and smash it. He had more than once thought of contacting Lester in the Home Office – or Stanforth. It would have been easy to have excused himself to the Prime Minister by telling him the truth, but the PM would have acted on the information and Dee wouldn't have survived. Both Lester and Stanforth could be Group members. Jackson had made clear the extent of the infiltration. Although he was free to move around, he had no sense of freedom. He had been warned that he would be watched and it was no idle warning. There was nothing he could do for Dee other than wait for orders and try to carry them out. He had made a good job of the performance last night. The thought of Dee had given him the impetus to carry it through. A positive act to secure her release was better than trying to exist through the long hours of so-called normal living. Until he had heard the cassette his anxiety had been punctuated by periods of calm. Now he had none. Stress was as physical as a pain and worse in its effect. It blurred his judgment so that he couldn't think clearly any more. He hoped his performance next time would be adequate, whatever that performance might be.

SIX

On the fourteenth of April the Provisionals bombed a pub in Islington. On the sixteenth an Irish owned restaurant was bombed in reprisal. The identity of both bombings was perfectly clear. On the following Sunday an Israeli aeroplane exploded just after take-off – again the identity of the perpetrators was plain.

In a small semi-detached house in Hounslow the senior members of the Group sat around a circular teak table and discussed timing. The Leader of the Nucleus, as the inner Committee was called, was pointing to a date in his diary. It was May the first. May Day. He turned to Admiral Jackson, 'You still think it's too soon?'

'I don't think Berringer has been sufficiently publicised yet. His own television performance went down well, but there should be others.'

'If there are others of the same kind he will be forced to resign from Parliament. If that happens we defeat our own ends and we risk losing a cross-section of the British public who equate our Parliamentary system with the Church of England and God.'

One of the other members, a former Secretary of State under a previous Government, laughed. 'You're right, of course. Berringer, the fallen angel. It wouldn't do. He represents the system and the people have to be weaned from it slowly.'

'Quite. After the take-over, his will be the familiar figure. He needs to stay unsullied.'

77

The Admiral interposed, 'I still think it's hurrying it. He could be brought before the public in a non-controversial way.'

'Such as?' The Leader showed his impatience.

'Some more publicity in *The Galaxy*. A series of lectures on non-inflammatory Parliamentary topics.'

There was a murmur of disagreement. The Leader voiced it, 'That sort of publicity would dull the edges of the man. He thumped the nation into awareness. The nation is alive to him . . . and, Berringer apart, I believe the time is right. In the last few days we've had the bonus of three bombings we've had nothing to do with. The mood of the people is very angry indeed. There have been scenes in Downing Street. Stones have been thrown through the windows of *The Times* offices because they presented a reasoned argument calling for restraint. Do you suppose we can fabricate such ideal circumstances at a later date – or, if we can, do you think the heat of the people's anger will be any greater? The public is conditioned to violence. They'll shout now and be malleable now, but if nothing is done they'll forget.' He turned to the short, thickset man seated on his left. 'What about you, Carling? You've studied Berringer's behaviour? What's your view as a psychiatrist? Is he ready? Will he conform?'

Carling gave the question some thought before replying. He knew Berringer socially rather than professionally and was wary of a shallow analysis. He answered in lay terms and believed he was as close to the truth as he could get. 'I can only repeat what I have already told you. I believe he will conform – eventually. By eventually I mean a year or more. He's a realist and he'll accept what has to be accepted and he'll make the best of it. He's basically honest and for a while it will jar him to go against what he thinks of as his principles. He's worked well for the people in the context of democracy, because he believes in democracy. He'll work equally well under our system once he's come to terms with it. Until he comes to terms with it he will do what we force him to do. He did

78

that broadcast under heavy pressure and he did it splendidly. I believe he'll continue to do whatever we tell him provided he's worried about his wife. Obviously that pressure can only be exerted for a limited time. Either she is returned to him or she isn't. If she is held for too long I think the strain will be too much for him and he will perform less well. If she is returned then he won't perform at all.'

'So what's your answer?'

'I think May Day would suit excellently, but there must be continuing pressure – of one sort of another – and it must be of a kind that involves him absolutely. Holding Mrs Berringer has a limited time value – there must be something more.'

The only woman member of the Nucleus spoke for the first time. She was a statistician, middle-aged and plumply pretty.

'Well,' she said hesitantly, 'there is only one way that would maximise his involvement and hold him to us totally and forever through the sheer depth of his guilt.'

The others looked at her and waited.

'He could,' she said, 'be the one to plant the bomb.'

SEVEN

Dee was pegging out sheets on a makeshift line when Admiral Jackson paid his visit to the cottage. This time it was without secrecy and had the overtones of a social occasion. It was a pleasant morning with a sharp breeze blowing sun-gilded clouds across the sky. He left his car at the bottom of the track and walked briskly taking in deep lungsful of air.

The Berringer woman, as he thought of her, looked rather splendid standing up there against the sky-line with the sheets billowing about her. The wind was blowing her fine dark hair all over the place and she had an untidy peasant-like quality he hadn't seen in her before. He wondered if she would remember him. He had known Berringer for years, but had had very little contact with her. Their last meeting had been at a dinner-party given by a mutual friend. She had been exquisitely groomed. Put together, his wife had said cattily, with the most tremendous care.

There was a movement in the high grass to the left of him and he saw that the dog mounted guard. She, too, became aware of the movement and looked around warily.

At first she thought he was a stranger approaching and then she realized who he was. As he got closer to her he saw the changing expressions on her face. She was surprised to see him. She was glad that someone from the outside world was there. She was wondering

81

why he was there. She was hoping to God he had come to take her away.

She was quite incapable for several seconds of greeting him.

'Good morning, Mrs Berringer.'

A sheet loose at one end flapped madly. He recovered the peg from where it had blown in the grass and handed it to her smiling.

She took it – looked at it as if she didn't know what it was – and then clumsily pegged the sheet.

'Admiral Jackson.'

'That's right. I wondered if you would remember me.'

'Of course I remember you. You're one of David's friends.' It came out slowly, almost painfully, as if she hardly dared voice the hope. 'You've come to take me to him. It's finished. It's going to be all right.'

He wondered if Mackilroy had told her that he was a member of the Group or whether she had some strange telepathic gift that told her it was so. And then he realized that she thought no such thing. She saw him as someone from the other side of the fence. The respectable, normal, everyday side where she and David played domesticated harmonies and fiddled their harmless tunes.

He disabused her of the idea, but gently. 'No, I'm afraid it's not that simple. May we go inside and talk?'

Disappointment seemed to diminish her physically so that she drooped with fatigue and then she made an effort and became artificially a hostess. 'Of course.' She walked at his side and then preceded him into the cottage. Her eyes apologized for the untidyness of the room and then she shrugged and offered him a chair.

'You've been busy.' He referred to the pile of washed clothes ready for sorting on the table.

She smiled wryly. 'I get manic periods of activity when I feel I must do something – and then I do too much. You know the circumstances – why I'm here – of course?'

'Yes, but for interest, why do you assume I should?'

'Because nobody in his right mind would visit this God forsaken place without a valid reason. It would be too much to expect that you came merely for lunch.'

'It would.'

'And so?'

'And so we have time and needn't rush anything.' He took out his cheroot case. 'May I?'

'Please do.'

She sat and watched him. 'Did you tell Mack you were coming?'

'Why should you think that?'

She didn't know. She had a growing feeling of collusion between him and Mack. He was waiting for an answer and she tried to give him one. 'He goes into the barn every day between nine and nine-thirty. There's a transmitter there. He doesn't allow me in – or rather, the dog doesn't. You could have told him you were coming.' She added almost apologetically. 'When I mentioned Mack you didn't ask who he was, you countered it with another question. Obviously you know each other.'

She would be more in her element, he thought, dispensing tea for him from a silver teapot. Being inquisitorial embarrassed her.

He agreed blandly. 'Yes, I was in touch with Mackilroy earlier. He came down to the village less than half an hour ago. We met there.'

She nodded, growing realization beginning to lie on her like a pall. Oddly she felt little surprise. That Mack himself should be sufficiently aberrated to belong to a terrorist organization she had learnt to take. If he could belong then so could anybody including this silver-haired, suave, eminent man of the sea. She was living in a world gone mad. Like Alice in the forbidden garden nothing was what it seemed.

At last she put it into words. 'And so you are the one who is holding David.'

'I am a member of the Group which we are persuading David to join.'

And then he told her – all of it. Or almost all of it. The final act of commitment he still withheld.

Her composure as she listened was complete. David's performance on the television had lain at the back of her mind for some while now. It was obvious that pressure was being exerted, he would never have behaved like that otherwise. She had no deep feeling for politics. If David had wanted to change his Party she wouldn't have cared. But to be forced to bend his views to suit a group of megalomaniacs trying to introduce a power-based oligarchy was quite another matter. Despite a plausible presentation of the case the Admiral had failed to justify either his philosophy or his method of implementing it. Had she been held hostage to spring a prisoner from gaol she could have understood and even felt some sympathy. But to be held prisoner so that they could have power over David's deeply held political principles was something else again.

The Admiral, realizing that he had met a wall of resistance, tried another approach. 'I understand you are extremely proud of your husband. And rightly so. He is a man of rare qualities. Under the new system he will make a wonderful leader. The people already know him. They trust him. He represents the best in the old system. The metamorphosis from the old to the new will be acceptable to them when he makes it clear that it is acceptable to him.'

'But it isn't.'

'But it will be.' The Admiral leaned forward a little in his chair and his eyes showed something of his fanaticism though his voice was cool. 'We are not offering evil in exchange for good. We are offering order and intelligent leadership in exchange for chaos bordering on anarchy. Even the best of the new is always regarded with suspicion. David has been programmed by his upbringing. He follows the rules he knows, but in time the prejudice will go.'

84

'And you honestly think you can re-programme him against his will?'

'No – he can be made to perform under duress – but the re-programming will come when he wants it to come and that will happen when he realizes that the system is working not only working well but working for the common good. He will re-programme himself.'

'I don't believe you.'

The Admiral smiled. 'Naturally not. You and your husband are cast in the same mould. Besides which the idea has only just been presented to you. You are rejecting it without thought – just as he did. But you saw his television performance, I believe? Did you notice how his earlier hesitancy developed into a strongly worded criticism of the status quo? Do you think he would have been so convincing if the spark of a new belief wasn't there?'

'He acted the part well because you forced him to.'

'Do you suppose we would have forced him to do anything if we weren't utterly convinced that he was the right man for us? He knows it subconsciously though he would deny it vigorously. In time he will admit to the truth.'

She shook her head.

'Then let me try to prove it to you on another level.' He took out a notebook and a ball-point pen. 'Are you ambidextrous?'

'No.' The question surprised her.

'Do you write with your right hand or with your left?'

'With my right.'

'If you wrote with your left hand the writing would have all the characteristics of your right hand, but it would be more clumsy, isn't that so?'

'Yes – naturally.'

'But in time – if you practised – what you wrote with your left hand would be as clear and distinct as what you wrote with your right. It would, however, take will-power. It would have to seem necessary to take the trouble. An emotional motivation as well as an intellectual one would speed the process.'

He tore out a sheet of paper from the notebook and wrote 'David' laboriously with left hand. 'I think we can say fairly that my interest in David is an intellectual one. Yours, however, is both intellectual and emotional. Write his name with your left hand and see how your effort differs from mine.' He handed her a fresh piece of paper and the pen.

Convinced now that he must be mad, but deciding to humour him, she did as he said. The name looked like a child's clumsy effort – or a maimed person's effort – or the effort of someone too weak to write normally.

The Admiral compared it with his own writing and then took it from her. He wasn't an accomplished sophist and found it difficult to carry the argument through. 'I believe it would take less time and effort for your writing to become clear than it would mine. Once David becomes clear about his attitudes and is prepared to forgo his prejudices, his left hand – his learning hand – will equal his right. In other words his loyalty to the new will equal what he felt previously for the old system.' With apparent casualness he folded up the paper she had written on and put it in his notecase. It had, he felt, been an extremely civilized meeting and he had gained everything he wanted without the slightest degree of unpleasantness. She was, he believed, a complete fool.

She said bluntly, 'You're not going to let me go, are you?'

'Eventually – yes. Not today. I came today to explain our aims to you. Think about what I've told you. Talk about it with Mackilroy. In time you'll be standing at David's side, sharing his new beliefs, helping to build a country to be proud of.'

'Hallelujah!' It was a sharp, hard, explosion of anger and took him completely by surprise.

She stood up and blazed at him. 'You have the nerve to come here and preach idealized poppycock to me. You offer the country order – you say – and you bomb a restaurant. You corrupt decent men like Mack so that they perform like gangsters. How do you suppose we feel about each other now – he and I? He's holding me here and it's against his nature to do it, but he's doing it because you and your lot have *programmed him* – wouldn't *brainwashed* be better? And you think you can make David throw every belief he's ever held overboard – not by persuasion – or honest argument, because you can't argue honestly – but by holding me. What have you told him? That I'm living it up with Mack – that we spend all the goddamned days and nights in bed? Are you getting at him through pain and jealousy? Or if not that – what? Have you told him you'll do me in if he doesn't do what you want him to do?' She halted in mid-spate, clearly and dreadfully sure that she had just spoken the truth.

She looked at him white-faced waiting for a denial, but he was already walking through the door.

Mack, too, had left his van at the bottom of the track. The Admiral's request for time on his own with Dee had filled him with disquiet. He didn't seriously believe that Jackson intended the girl any physical harm, but the episode with the rat had shown a side to his nature that was both surprising and shocking. It seemed wise to be quietly around.

The Admiral, quick to interpret Mackilroy's presence near the cottage, decided not to comment on it. As a jailer he did well enough. The emotional overtones added an interesting element that might be useful. He might eventually be able to persuade Mrs Berringer to overcome her prejudices, but if he didn't . . . The Admiral looked at him thoughtfully. 'You and she . . . you're not getting along too well?'

Mack said crisply, 'Under the circumstances that's not surprising.'

'Do you want to withdraw from the assignment?'

It was odd to describe Dee as an assignment. 'No.'

'But she's not offering you the pleasures of her bed.' It was a statement made to needle out a reaction.

Mack held on to his cool. 'Is that what you talked about? I thought you intended telling her about the Group. You mentioned a letter of persuasion she might write to her husband.'

'About which you were sceptical.'

'I know her.'

'That's what we're banking on.'

They were walking down the track towards the two cars and at the bottom of the field they stopped. The air was sweet and heavy with the scent of blackthorn. 'As a hideaway for young lovers,' the Admiral said, 'what could be more perfect?' His voice was like honey on a sharp knife.

Mack's expression didn't alter. 'Did she write the letter?'

'No.'

'I thought she wouldn't.'

'As I said before,' the Admiral said pleasantly, 'you know her so well.' He got into his car and wound down the window. 'You have eight days with her, Mackilroy – until the first of May.'

'The first of May . . . you mean D Day?'

'If we must use old-fashioned terms – yes.' The Admiral proceeded to give him the details, but selectively and only those that were relevant to him.

Before returning to the cottage Mack took a walk around the fields. May Day in this particular year of grace wouldn't be celebrated by coloured ribbons around a maypole – not even the coloured ribbons of party politics. The central pole of government would be split from top to bottom. Now that the countdown had begun he felt a degree of euphoria. A lark, high up and out of sight, let out a bubble of sound like champagne bubbles breaking. He threw back his head and searched the sky for the bird and saw only small drifts of cloud. Momentarily sunblinded he rubbed his knuckles against his eyes.

Eight days.

Eight days seen now through a mist of excitement.

The cottage in contrast to the brightness of the day seemed dark when he returned to it. He couldn't see Dee's face as clearly as she saw his. She was ironing and after a quick glance at him the iron lingered too long on a pillow case and began to singe it. He took the iron from her and upended it. 'You were scorching it.'

She didn't answer.

'So Admiral Jackson put you in the picture.'

'If that's what you call it.' She tried to remember the name of the artist whose schizoid pictures of hell had terrified her when she saw them as a child.

There was a quality in her voice that hadn't been there before. He had become used to her irritability and boredom, but now there was something else.

He tried to explore her mood. 'You were shocked and surprised by what he told you?'

'Wouldn't you expect me to be?'

'The Group is working for the common good.'

'Oh, yes.' It was very dry.

He tried to put it to her using his personal viewpoint. 'You've lived in your own small privileged world. What goes on outside it has touched you very little. You've read about it in the papers. You've heard about it on the radio. You've seen it on the television. It's there outside somewhere – going on. Not nice, you say, as you sit back in your chair. Not nice, at all. And then for a while you stop reading, listening, looking. You pick up a novel. You turn the knob and listen to Mozart. You switch programmes and watch a play. It doesn't touch you. Not as it touched me. As a journalist I was in it. I not only saw the napalm, I smelt the burning skin.'

'Napalm – not here. You're talking of another country.'

'Not here – not yet. But when?'

'Evil doesn't stop evil. Violence doesn't stop violence. The Silver Swan . . .'

'An unfortunate necessity.'

'And other unfortunate necessities – do you know, that sounds almost unctuous. Where did you get the phrase from – the Gestapo? Is that what they told their victims before they applied torture – an unfortunate necessity.'

He was able to see her more clearly now that his eyes were adjusting to the room. Her pallor worried him. 'What did Jackson say to you?'

'More or less what you are saying to me.'

'He asked you to write to David to try to persuade him to comply – but you wouldn't.'

'Is that what he told you?'

'Isn't it true?'

She took up the pillow case, carefully folded it into four, and then dropped it crumpled onto the table. 'He got me to write the name David with my left hand. I don't know why he wanted it. I don't know why I did it. You know, don't you? Tell me why.'

He wanted to be in the sun again. He wanted to recapture the mood of loyalty to a creed that had so recently been excitingly and unequivocally desirable.

Oh yes, he knew.

But he couldn't tell her.

She came over to where he was standing by the window. 'Well?'

'I don't know.'

She felt bereft as if he had finally walked away.

He reached out and touched her hand. It was like ice.

'Mack – let me go.'

'Can't I even touch you now?' There was pain in his voice, but the misunderstanding was deliberate.

'You know what I mean. Will you let me leave here?'

'In time – yes.'

'Now.'

'No.'

'I see. You really are committed, aren't you?' She tried to keep her voice steady, but he recognized the undertone for what it was. She had become afraid – not only of the situation – but of him.

Appalled, he turned from her abruptly and left the room.

EIGHT

When Briony was happy she sang tuneless little ditties that grated on David's already stretched nerves. Her moods went up and down like a cable-car. The odd bursts of song happened during her domesticated moments when she was briefly too fully occupied to think about anything. In the evenings she brooded and he avoided her as much as he could. She was obsessional about blindness. The fact that the bomb she had planted had killed, she was somehow better able to accept than the fact that one of the victims had lost the sight of one eye.

David, coming home one evening after dark, had found her seated in the darkened study. She had looked up at him startled when he switched on the light. He knew why she sat there. There was a growing rapport between them. He resented it, but he couldn't deny it.

He said sharply. 'Economising?'

'What?'

'Afraid that I'll ask you to settle the electricity bill?'

'Don't be silly.'

She wanted to be comforted. He took some papers out of his briefcase, ignoring her.

She said, 'I didn't hear you coming in.'

'The hall is carpeted. I don't wear hobnailed boots.'

'Do you think that one's other senses become stronger if

one loses one of one's senses?'

He was impatient. 'One's this – one's that. Can he hear better now that he can't see – that's what you're asking, isn't it?'

'Can't see . . . do you mean the other eye has gone?'

He had read about it in the paper. The man was now totally blind.

She interpreted his silence. 'Oh, God!' She was aghast. 'Oh, God – no!'

He looked at her uneasily. An asthmatical attack on top of the pressure of the day allied to his ever present worry about Dee would be the final straw to break his self-control.

She began to cry.

Her tears were bearable.

He sat through them and waited until they were spent.

She said at last, 'I'm sorry . . . I mean I'm sorry for unloading my conscience on to you.'

'You can't. Your conscience is your own affair.'

'Yes. But in a little way it's yours. You know what I'm feeling. You pretend you don't, but you do.' Her face was wet and blotchy and unlovely. A tear, motionless in the angle of her jaw, reflected the light. He resisted the temptation to reach over and wipe it away.

He said, 'We're forced to live together. There's bound to be an awareness.'

That night he noticed that she slept with her bedroom light on – if she slept. He lay in the darkness and thought of Dee. Briony, in her involvement with the Group, was responsible for whatever happened to Dee. His condemnation of her should be pitiless. Should be? Was.

And yet . . .

The next morning he heard her singing in the bathroom. So she had slept after all – probably better than he had. He had spent most of the night trying to find a way out of the morass, but there wasn't a way. Dee's freedom rated higher than his political freedom. He couldn't have both.

He waited until she had quitted the bathroom and then he went in to take his bath. She had used Dee's talcum and the subtle perfume permeated his senses so that by closing his eyes he imagined Dee there. The bath wet after Dee. Dee's footprints on the mat. Anger with Briony suffused him and when he went down to the kitchen she sensed it and broke off in mid-song.

She didn't ask him what was wrong. It was the perfume. She had been a fool to use it. Once when she was a child she had seen a farmer put the skin of a dead lamb on a living one so that the ewe would accept it. The situation here was quite different, but the rejection was the same. She asked him calmly what he wanted to eat.

'Nothing – just coffee.'

'You can't spend the day in the House with nothing inside you.' That, too, she knew was a mistake. Dee's perfume. Now Dee's role of domesticity. She shrugged. 'All right. Have it your own way.'

She began to sing again, but out of bravado this time, her eyes wary.

'Briony, why don't you quit?'

She knew he didn't mean the singing. 'You mean – leave you? I can't. I have my orders.'

'I mean quit the Group.'

'I can't.'

'Can't or won't?'

She answered it honestly. 'Both. I believe in the Group. But even if I didn't I couldn't quit at this stage – it wouldn't be possible.'

'It could be, if I helped you. If you'd give me names, I'd know who I could safely go to for help.'

'We've been over all this before. I haven't that sort of knowledge – and even if I had, I wouldn't. Not even for you.'

There was a softness in her voice as she spoke the last few words, and he looked at her, perturbed.

The House didn't sit until half-past two. He needed to catch up

95

on his constituency work, but knew he wouldn't be able to put his mind to it. These days he was delegating more and more of his responsibilities and his staff was beginning to look askance at him. The rumour was spreading that he had marital problems. A couple of invitations had come through for himself and Dee which he had had to decline. His colleagues tended to regard him with sympathetic curiosity and, afraid of being asked unanswerable questions, he had kept as far as possible out of their way. He hoped that whatever was going to happen would happen soon. He felt like a pariah in the wilderness.

When he told Briony he intended taking the morning off, she was worried. 'You mean you're not going to work? But won't they wonder where you are?'

'They' were to Briony a faceless group of Civil Servants.

'Possibly. It doesn't matter.'

'For a paragon of political virtues, don't you think your behaviour rather odd?' The barb was back in her voice and he was glad of it.

'Perhaps I'm not such a paragon of political virtues after all – try telling your mob.'

'Where are you going and what are you going to do? If you're thinking of trying to make contact with anyone, don't.'

He wasn't. He was going to take the car out of London and drive as far as he could in any direction in the time permitted. He told her so.

She drummed her fingers on the table top in a gesture of exasperation. 'You were told to carry on your duties as normal. That means going to work.'

'I shall attend the House this afternoon.'

'Oh, bully for you, you will attend the House this afternoon! What happens if someone from the House phones you this morning?'

'You'll just have to cope, won't you?'

Her knew very well that her way of coping was to put the phone down immediately she knew she couldn't cope. At best the callers regarded her as an au-pair girl with a poor knowledge of the language. At worst they believed he consoled himself during Dee's absence.

She saw a way out of the dilemma. 'I'll come with you.'

'Oh no, you won't. Your job is to stay here and sweat it out, so here you'll stay.'

'My job is to see that you do what you've been told to do – and if you won't, then my job is to stay with you and see that you don't do anything stupid. Wait for me while I go and borrow one of Dee's coats.'

He was walking down the street to where his car was parked when he heard her running footsteps. Much smaller in stature than Dee, the too-large blue coat flapped around her legs and made her look ridiculous.

He told her brutally to go back to the flat, that he didn't want her, but she refused to listen. 'If you don't let me come with you, I'll make a scene here on the pavement. Don't you see I've got to come?' The scene was no idle threat and there were plenty of curious passers-by to take notice of it.

He gave way irritably. 'All right – but get into the back seat. And if you start talking I'll stop the car and throw you out.'

'As from now, I won't say a word.'

He drove south of the Thames and when he was approaching Dulwich he became convinced that he was being tailed. The white Volvo had kept its distance for the past half hour but had never at any time been out of sight. He tried one or two sideroads off Lordship Lane and it was still there.

He was the first to break the silence. 'One of your friends?'

'The white car? Possibly.'

'Surely, you know.'

'How could I? The Group isn't like a little local club where everybody knows everybody. You keep letting the name mislead you. Army would denote the numbers better, only it isn't just a military organization.'

'But includes a substantial number of army personnel?'

'I don't know.' She hesitated, 'Yes, of course it does, why deny it.'

It seemed pointless to drive further out and he drew the car up at the gates of Dulwich Park. He and Dee had gone boating there once and had fed the ducks. It seemed a lifetime away.

He told Briony he was going to take a walk. 'On my own. Amuse your friend in the white Volvo when he shows up.'

She said something about needing fresh air, too.

Four young boys were playing tennis and he sat and watched them. They played with great concentration and no skill. The balls were yellow. One of the balls lobbed over the netting and Briony who was walking up caught it and threw it back. The boy shouted his thanks.

Briony said, 'Wouldn't it be nice if this were life. I mean just ordinary things. Yellow tennis balls. The smell of grass. Will you let me sit down beside you?'

'Where is your friend in the white car?'

'He's on the other side of the park. I expect he'll be with us when we drive away.'

'What would happen if I approached him and asked him what the hell he wanted?'

'He'd probably smile politely at you and ask you if you were out of your mind.'

And that, David thought, would be the simple solution to the whole set-up. It wasn't happening. He was demented to think it was. In a moment or two Dee would approach him along the path and they would take one of those boats over there again. The swan would glide up out of the reeds and she would trail her fingers in the soft small waves that followed it. Later they would go up to the inn and sit at one of the garden tables. She would drink gin and lime and he would have beer. There would be the sound of young children playing.

He felt the touch of a hand on his. 'Don't look like that.'

'I wish you hadn't worn Dee's coat.' It was a defensive response, equal to a slap.

'I wish I hadn't, too, but I haven't one with me. It's too cold to be without.' It was several minutes before she spoke again. 'There's an aviary over there.'

'Yes.'

'Will you come and watch the birds with me? Or did you and Dee watch the birds, too?'

Her perceptiveness was uncanny. Or was the dossier on him so complete that they even knew that?

'Go and watch them on your own.'

'You won't drive away without me?'

'No.'

He watched her as she walked up to the enclosure. She looked like an adolescent on a day's outing. The birds really interested her. She poked her fingers through the wire netting and made chirping noises at them. When she rejoined him she was smiling. 'Their colours are beautiful. I painted a picture of a parakeet once and I sold it.' She waited for him to comment and when he didn't she shrugged. 'Don't you want to know how much I sold it for?'

'Tell me if you must.'

'Not if you don't want to know.'

'You'll probably tell me anyway.'

'Five pounds.'

'Not a lot.'

'A lot when you're only fifteen. I bought myself more paints with it. One day I'll go to art school. That's what I've always wanted to do – go and study art.'

He looked at her in astonishment. That she was walking freely

99

now was due to the ineptitude of the police and his own inability to turn her in.

He wondered if he would if he could.

'What are you thinking about, David?'

'About you – what an extraordinary person you are.'

'In what way?'

He didn't want to blight the moment by telling her. It occurred to him that the man in the white Volvo might be a police officer, in which case her period of happiness would be short.

She said astutely, 'You're worried. About me?'

He wished he could undo her actions of the last few months, like unzipping a dress that she could step out of and kick aside. He wished he could make her a present of peace of mind.

On the return journey to Kensington the white Volvo was replaced by a black Morris Minor of ancient vintage – or perhaps it was just going in the same direction. He gave up bothering about it. Briony, seated beside him now, suggested they should lunch out. 'It will be quicker. If you're to be at the House by two-thirty I won't have time to cook you anything.'

He hesitated. 'Should you be seen around – I mean, in a public place?'

At first she didn't understand, and then she did. 'You think that someone from the Silver Swan might see me and recognize me?'

'It's more than possible.'

'And you mind . . .? I mean you mind for my sake . . . not just because of what might happen to Dee?'

'I didn't say that.' His motives were too mixed for him to be able to give a clear answer. 'If you are pulled in, I can hardly be blamed for it. It shouldn't rate as non-compliance. It shouldn't bounce back on Dee.'

'It wouldn't be fair, would it?' She was amused now, teasing him. 'Don't worry. We'll eat out at a French restaurant I know just two streets away from the flat. I won't be pulled in.'

'Because the restaurateur will mount an armed guard over you – or because the Group has the police in its pocket?'

She chuckled. 'You almost smiled then, do you know that? I'm glad you're worried about me. It puts flesh on my bones – makes me feel nice.'

The restaurant made a fetish of discretion with its dim lights and quiet alcoves. He thought the whole set-up in appalling taste, but the food was reasonable.

She asked, 'You've never been here with Dee?'

'No.'

She thought, thank God for that. 'What shall we talk about?'

Anxiety had killed his appetite since he had heard the cassette, but the roast duck was good and he managed to eat most of his portion of it. 'Must we talk?'

'No, I suppose not. Let's have a comfortable silence.'

'Comfortable?'

'By just concentrating on being here now, forgetting everything else.'

'And can you forget?'

'If you'll let me – just for a little while.' She was pleading. 'Please . . .'

He didn't know how to answer her. She had taken Dee's coat off and folded it behind her. Her arms looked thinner than ever and there were blobs of freckles on her shoulders. She had a lost uncared-for look like a child who had been kicked out of the parental home and didn't know which way to go. At this particular moment it was difficult to believe her capable of terrorism. At this particular moment he felt traitorously aware of her sexually. It was in her moments of weakness that he wanted her. After the asthmatical attack. Now. Dee had never had that effect on him. With her, sexual awareness came more strongly when she was at her most beautiful.

She understood him. 'Do you have to go to the House this afternoon?'

101

He understood her. 'It's Thursday. The Leader of the House presents the programme for the following week.'

'Which makes it a greater priority. Would you put your Parliamentary commitments first if it were Dee?'

'It is Dee.' He stood up and beckoned the waiter over. 'It's Dee all the time . . . and that, for me, is quite unforgettable.'

She sat at the table for some time after he had left and went over the morning again in her mind. His attraction for her was more than physical. It was an admission that she was afraid to make to herself, but it was true. She wanted to sleep with him and he – occasionally – wanted to sleep with her. For him it was sex and nothing more. Or was it? In his condemnation of her he used harsh words harshly, but his eyes betrayed a reluctant compassion. She had killed and that put her beyond the pale. The fact that she had killed unwittingly made the crime a degree less heinous. He was beginning to mind for her sake that she had done it. A few days ago if the police had come knocking at the door he would have handed her over with relief. Now? She didn't know. He probably didn't know himself.

She tried to see him objectively as the Group saw him. A kind, dependable, intelligent man with enough fire in his veins to lift him above the ordinary. A good choice. He inspired confidence. He was easy to identify with. Under the new regime when he was finally committed to it he would lead the people quietly and with strength.

When he was finally committed to it.

The method of forcing his commitment had always seemed to her grotesque. And yet it was working. In his television performance he had been like a swimmer swimming against the tide and then turning, slowly at first, and going with it. He had ended on the crest of a wave. There was probably something of an actor in all successful politicians and perhaps he was a better actor than most . . . but for one or two brief moments towards the end he hadn't seemed to be acting at all.

But perhaps that was wishful thinking.

With the hit men of the Group twisting his arm through Dee, his performance didn't dare to be less than brilliant. Dee's screams on the cassette had been appalling. She hadn't believed that Dee would be physically hurt when Mack had taken her hostage. She had never liked Mack very much, but she hadn't believed him capable of inflicting violence or standing by and watching it. Admiral Jackson's complicity was equally shocking. During all the years she had known him he had condemned brutality and yet now he was party to it. There was a growing resentment in her – particularly against him. Her father had been one of his junior officers during his sea-going days and by coincidence the two families had lived within a few miles of each other. When her father had been killed, the Admiral had stepped in and helped in all practical ways. He had been easy to talk to and she had been easy to mould. The hit and run driver had become for her the embodiment of lawlessness and lawlessness was now the spreading evil of the country. The Group was the panacea.

But the panacea had a bitterness that lay in her stomach like gall. She hadn't known it was going to be like this. The bomb – a small one, they told her – would hurt no-one. Dee's abduction, they told her, would be a pleasant time for Dee. She was going with her lover, wasn't she? Berringer would be motivated partly by jealousy and partly by doubt as to what was actually happening to her. The last part they hadn't explained, and she hadn't pressed for an explanation. The tape eventually had made it clear.

She had talked earlier to David with a degree of bravado about blood on the banner of idealism. The blood of the people shed for the good of the cause was like carmine paint on an artist's palette. It didn't mean very much. Just words. The dead of the Silver Swan came off the palette and touched her. Dee's voice on the cassette rang in her ears. Not all the time, but enough of the time to take the shine out of the sun.

She got up abruptly and put on Dee's coat. Despite its weight and

103

warmth she felt cold in it. It carried a faint smell of tweed and the smell repelled her. Even when she left the restaurant and walked in the fresh air the smell lay heavily on her chest so that she found it increasingly hard to breathe. It was odd, she thought, that she hadn't noticed it when she was in the car and in the park. David's presence, reluctant as it was, was healing.

NINE

The security of the Group was tight. Sybil Atkinson as a senior member of the Nucleus knew that the girl approaching the flat was Briony, a protegée of Admiral Jackson, and according to Jackson an excellent choice for the job of being around Berringer and keeping an eye on the domestic front. Briony, however, had never seen Sybil Atkinson before.

She thought at first that she was David's sister, Sally. There was a similarity between the two women seen at a distance. They were both short, plump and fair. On closer inspection the similarity ended. This woman exuded a quiet authority. Her dark brown eyes showed an uncomfortable awareness.

'Should you be out, Briony?'

Briony, startled that the other woman knew her, tried to slot her into the right compartment of acquaintances and failed.

'Should I be out? Why shouldn't I be out? Who are you?'

'A colleague of Admiral Jackson's.'

Briony's attitude of natural belligerence changed perceptibly. 'You'd better come in.'

She took the other woman through into the sitting-room. Sybil Atkinson looked around her with approval. It was a pleasant room full of greens and browns and with good pieces of antique furniture carefully chosen. The girl, she thought, looked out of her element in it. She had taken off the coat that so obviously wasn't hers and

105

thrown it on the back of a chair. Her red tank top and brown slacks looked grubby.

She answered the question Briony had put to her. 'The police are still working on the Silver Swan bombing. You were told to lie low here in the flat.'

Briony answered sulkily. 'I can't stay in forever – I haven't been far.'

'To Dulwich this morning – and then to a restaurant. That wasn't wise.'

Briony shrugged. David had been right about the white Volvo. And someone had been in the restaurant, too. It was to be expected. This woman, she supposed, had come to give her a ticking-off. If she were to stay on the job, she had better hang on to her temper.

'When he insisted on taking the car I thought I had better go with him.'

'He' sounded impersonal, instinct told her to try to keep it that way.

'What happens outside the flat is the responsibility of other people. How are you getting on together?'

'It could be worse.'

The other woman's eyes seemed to bore into her. 'What's the matter? Have you a cold?'

Briony tried to control her breathing. 'Nothing much. A chest cold.'

Sybil accepted the explanation. 'You didn't bring any extra clothes with you. That showed lack of forethought. You could have carried a rucksack in Mackilroy's van. How did Berringer react to your wearing his wife's coat?'

'Not very well.'

'I'm not surprised. I'll arrange for a suitcase of your clothes to be packed and sent around. How is he reacting generally?'

'He's fond of his wife. How would you expect him to react?' The belligerence was back. She couldn't help it.

'I'm asking you. You're with him all the time. Does he talk about her?'

'Not very much.'

'Because he's antagonistic towards you or because he finds it too painful to talk about?'

'Both.'

'Would you say he was deeply in love with his wife?'

The words, Briony thought, sounded incongruous coming from that fat complacently pretty face.

'Yes.' She tried to make the reply dead-pan, if only her bloody chest didn't hurt so.

'Earlier you said fond of – but, in fact, it's something stronger? To say he's deeply in love is not exaggerating?'

'No.'

'How did he react when he heard Mrs Berringer on the cassette?'

'Violently.'

'In what way?'

'He broke the cassette.'

'I see.' Sybil sat down and leaned back against the cushions. The Admiral had been wise to leave the cassette to Briony. She might be wise to do the same with the letter. She resisted the temptation.

'Tell me about him. Daily routine. Everything.'

Briony began to prowl the room. She picked up an onyx cigarette box and put it down again. 'He gets up at seven – baths – cleans his teeth – this is damned silly.'

'You may think so – go on.'

'I make breakfast. We have it on the kitchen table.'

'Why not in the dining room?'

'Because I can't be bothered to carry it through.'

'What about the shopping?'

'The deep freeze is well stocked.'

'I know he has put it about that you're an au-pair girl – did that idea originate from you or from him?'

107

'From his sister – she assumed it.'

'Other people see the relationship differently. Do you sleep with him?'

'Good God, no!' It came out explosively. She hoped not too explosively, but the other woman seemed satisfied.

'Let's carry on. You serve him breakfast – on the kitchen table. Do you eat together?'

'Sometimes. Sometimes he only wants coffee.'

'Why? Because he's slept badly? Is too worried to eat? Why?' Briony was getting bored with the inquisition. 'I don't know.'

'Doesn't he confide in you at all?'

'No.'

'You must talk about something – what do you talk about?'

'He wants me to tell him the names of people in the Group.'

'And what do you say to that?'

'I tell him I don't know. And I don't. At least not many and no-one important apart from the Admiral – and Mackilroy.'

'Does he talk to you about Mackilroy?'

'No.'

'What would you say his feelings are towards Mackilroy?'

'Ambivalent. Jealous of him because of what Dee felt for him. Angry with him because he didn't feel strongly enough for her to protect her from whatever made her scream.'

Sybil looked at the girl with a new respect. She was more percipient than she had suspected. Perhaps she was a good choice after all.

'All right, Briony – go on. We know what happens when he leaves here for the House of Commons. Now tell me what happens when he comes home.'

'He takes his brief case into the study and carries on working.'

'How do you know he works?'

'What else would he do?'

'Sits and broods, perhaps. You tell me.'

108

'I bring in a tray of tea. He sits at his desk and works.'

'Do you make an evening meal for him?'

'Yes. We have it at seven.'

'Sybil smiled faintly. 'In the kitchen?'

'Why not? It hardly merits polished mahogany and the best silver.'

'Does he complain about living very differently with you from the way he lived with his wife?'

'Good heavens, no! The man is worried sick. He's not bothered about trivialities.'

Sybil was beginning to hear what she had hoped to hear. 'You say he's worried sick. How do you know?'

'Well, wouldn't anybody be?'

'Does he talk about it?'

'No.'

'Does he reminisce about his wife?'

'No.'

'Because of his antagonism towards you?'

'Is that so surprising? After all I am a Group member.' It came out bitterly and she saw the other woman raise an eyebrow. She retrieved herself. 'We don't talk very much . . . about anything. Sometimes we play chess – but not often. He does *The Times* crosswords and he reads – or appears to.'

'You mean he shuts you out by appearing to be engrossed in a book?'

'Yes.'

'But he is in fact too much on edge to read?'

'Yes.'

'Who goes to bed first?'

'I do.'

'What time does he go?'

'It varies. Sometimes not until the early hours.'

'How do you know?'

109

'His bedroom light shines across the corridor into my room.'

'Aren't you a good sleeper?'

'Yes, but I don't sleep heavily. His light wakes me up and then I can't go to sleep until he puts it out.' She blanked her mind to the hours of wakefulness in case her face gave too much away. It was during the small hours that her need for his comfort was at its greatest.

'So you have disturbed nights, too?'

Briony was silent.

The other woman looked at her thoughtfully. The girl didn't look well, but that could be on account of her cold and her generally scruffy appearance. She asked her the same question that the Admiral had asked Mack.

'Do you want to stay on the assignment, Briony, or are you finding it too much of a strain?'

Briony felt her stomach give a lurch of apprehension. To live in a hell of her own making with David was better than living in that same hell on her own. She said brusquely, trying not to appear to care, 'I'm managing. I'd just as soon stay.'

Sybil said, 'Good. It won't be very long again now. We've had to bring everything forward. It's just a matter of days.'

She decided she might as well tell the girl. Berringer would be told it himself on his return from the House which would be sometime later that afternoon. Their contact from his department had told her that Berringer had a committee meeting at four, but it wasn't expected to last for more than an hour. He would be back at the flat at any time from five onwards unless he chose to take another walk along Westminster Bridge and he would hardly want to do that in the rush hour.

'And so,' she concluded, 'he'll know the terms of his wife's release this evening.'

It was a long time before Briony spoke and when she did, the words came out flatly. 'I'm sick. You must excuse me.' She got up

110

and walked carefully to the door. Her hands were slippery with sweat and she couldn't turn the knob. The other woman got up to help her. Shock took people in different ways, she supposed. Euphoria would be more in keeping with the nature of the news. Not that she wanted the girl to be euphoric – just level-headed and prepared to see everything through.

She chided her. 'I didn't expect such an emotional reaction from you. Are you sure you don't want to be replaced?'

'I've told you I'm sick. It's that time of the month. It's nothing whatever to do with . . .' She couldn't finish it. She turned and ran for the bathroom.

The committee meeting chaired by David broke up at four forty-five. That he could still function on one level while his thoughts were on another surprised him. Everything went smoothly almost as if invisible arms carried him effortlessly from A to B so that all he had to do was to sum up and close the meeting. He looked curiously at the faces around the table – faces he believed he knew so well. Responsible men in positions of authority. They looked back at him blandly. He stood up and scraped back his chair. Pruet, who had taken the minutes of the meeting in shorthand, closed his notebook and asked if there was anything more required of him that afternoon. David told him no. Pruet, trying to keep censure out of his voice, said that as he had not been able to attend that morning certain matters had had to be left in abeyance – did he want to advise on them now or would he wait until the morning? There was nothing urgent.

David said they could wait. The annunciator television screen showed that a debate was still going on in the Chamber which was half empty. The business didn't concern his department and it seemed pointless to go and sit in on it. He didn't particularly want to go home, either, but he couldn't think of anything else to do.

He let himself into the flat with his key and met Briony in the hall. She looked pinched and pale. He was about to ask her what was wrong when she forestalled him.

'You have a visitor.' She indicated the sitting-room. 'She wants to see you on your own.'

A wild lurching hope that it was Dee tore through him as he opened the door and then disappointment settled on him like a cloud. He had never seen the woman in his life before. She looked like one of his better heeled constituents – the sort that asked him to open fetes.

She gave him her true name, quite confidently, because the time for concealment had gone.

'I'm Sybil Atkinson. A statistician in the firm of Rogers and Liphook.'

She held out her hand and he shook it. A formal approach, he thought, one rarely shook hands these days. He wondered what the devil she wanted.

'Have we met – Mrs . . . er . . . Atkinson?'

'Miss. A widow, but I use my maiden name. No, we haven't met. I've followed your career with a lot of interest.'

He thought she probably wanted a subscription for something and asked her to be seated. He sat opposite her and hoped she would get her business over quickly.

'You're one of my constituents?'

'No.'

He noted that she had been smoking. The ash-tray on the small table by her chair was filled with the stubs of several cigarettes. He wondered how long she had been there.

She came straight to the point. 'I've come about your wife.'

Prepared for a period of polite non-talk leading up to something trivial, her directness arrowed him into attention.

'Dee? What about Dee? What's happening to her?'

Now that she had his attention she took her time to answer. The long manicured nail on her index finger touched a small brown mole

112

at the corner of her mouth as if to be assured that it was still there.

He watched her with mounting impatience.

She spoke at last. 'You know what's happening to her. And so do I. I'm shocked and I'm sorry. But I can't stop it happening. Only you can do that.'

'What do you mean?' The words calmly spoken masked everything he felt. He had spoken in the same even tones when the family doctor had told him that his mother had an inoperable cancer. The depth of his pain hadn't shown. And this was worse.

'I mean she's ill. Extremely weak.'

'And you're going to take me to her? You're going to allow her to come home?'

His quick acceptance of her as one of the Group disconcerted her. He had shown no surprise. The extent of his self-control disconcerted her even more.

'No, I'm sorry. I don't know where she is. I hope you'll believe that. It's true. I wouldn't have been entrusted with this message from her if I knew where she was.'

He had to suck his tongue to bring saliva into his mouth. 'A message from her?' He noticed the folded paper in the woman's hand.

'She was asked to write you a letter of persuasion, but . . . I'm sorry I have to say this . . . she – well, she was too weak – perhaps too hurt – I think there was some injury to her hand. This was all she could manage.' She handed the letter to him.

He looked down at it fearfully and saw his name. He saw everything he was supposed to see and he believed everything he was supposed to believe.

The woman seated opposite him was wearing a blue and green scarf. He wondered how long it would take her to die if he put it around her neck and strangled her. An eye for an eye.

She looked at him palely, half realizing what was in his mind, but had the courage to sit it out.

113

He was the first to turn away from her. He got up and went over to the window. There were cars passing. A furniture van and a taxi competed for a gap in the traffic. The taxi won. A dog fouled the pavement while its owner watched. An April shower flung a flurry of rain from a lavender sky.

He turned back to the room. 'What have they done to her?'

'I don't know. Believe me, I wasn't told.'

'Was it Mackilroy?'

'He's there, but I don't think he would be responsible.'

'But he didn't try to stop them.'

'Perhaps he couldn't. Only you can do that.'

'How?'

'By becoming a committed member of the Group.'

'Oh, for God's sake!' His rage was like a heavy surge of water against a dam. 'What more do you want of me. More rigged television programmes? An article boosting your insane image? Soap box oratory at Hyde Park corner? Or do you want me to catch the Speaker's eye at the House and declaim your virtues so loud and so clear that the Group will be invited to form a Fourth Party?'

'We want nothing of your democratic government. I thought you would have understood that by now.' She reached into her handbag and took out her cigarette case. He noticed that her hand was completely steady as she lit her cigarette. He would have been unable to light one for her.

'Then what the hell do you want?'

'We want you – but that you know already. The country needs you as their new leader – under our new regime.'

He felt as if he walked in Bedlam and could see no exit. This woman was mad. They were all mad. Just now he doubted his own sanity.

He said patiently as if he spoke to a very young child. 'There is no new regime. You're speaking of something impossible.'

'Nothing is impossible. Any historian can tell you that. Britain won the last war. That was impossible, but it happened.'

'We had right on our side.'

'That's pompous nonsense. You'll talk about God next and divine intervention.'

'What are you offering the country now – revolution?'

'It won't be necessary. The country will come with us. Democracy is effete and weak and England is dying under it. We offer strong leadership with military backing. The country needs it. The country, after the initial shock of the overthrow of the present system, will accept it.'

'And how do you propose to overthrow the present system?'

She looked at him through a haze of cigarette smoke, 'By striking at the very heart of government. By committing the ultimate outrage – an act of terrorism, supposedly perpetrated by any terrorist group the country cares to name.' He was a step ahead of her now. 'You mean – a bomb in the House of Commons?' His voice held amazed disbelief.

'Why not? It was tried in the United Nations building. The fact that it failed doesn't make it any less credible.'

He voiced it. 'You're mad.'

'Only failures are mad. We don't intend to fail.'

He felt as if he had walked a long way down a tortuous path that had somehow started with Dee. 'Why are you telling me this? Surely you know that I shall disclose everything to the Prime Minister. The security of the House will be tightened. The country will be combed for members of your Group. Jackson will be pulled in and made to talk.'

'And Mrs Berringer will die.'

The words fell like stones into a deep pond.

He was silent for a long time.

'A letter of persuasion – you said. What did you want her to write?'

'A plea for her life. A plea for your complete obedience.'

Obedience linked to a mythical future was sufficiently nebulous to seem not too demanding. What the Group planned to do couldn't happen. He was prepared to say anything.

'Very well, I'll give you my word to speak for you when the time comes.' When you're in the dock, he thought, and about to be sent down for life.

She smiled faintly. 'Stop thinking we're fools. Stop under-estimating us. We're not a little cranky band of idiots with a Guy Fawkes complex. We mean it. When we talk about your obedience we intend to make you so committed that you'll never be able to turn away.'

'You mean . . .?' He was too appalled to frame the question fully.

'Yes,' she said, 'who better? You know the security that already exists. You know the layout. We thought an adapted briefcase. You usually carry one. No-one will take any particular notice of it. You're a front bencher – so well placed. The details of the timing device will be given to you later. You'll have time to leave the Chamber before it happens. The element of doubt about it should salve your conscience. You're not pointing a gun at anyone. Some will live and some will die. You're not a selective executioner.' She stood up and pulled on a pair of pale grey gloves. 'You have to make a choice. If you do it, Mrs Berringer will live and so might the majority of parliamentarians there. If you don't do it then Mrs Berringer won't live. That's what I was told to tell you.' The look she gave him was tinged with pity. 'I'm sorry.'

'When is it to happen?' The question was almost academic. After the first shock of her words he was unnaturally calm again, as if a sword thrust had momentarily drawn blood and at the same time severed a nerve.

'In three days time – on the first of May. Your wife has three days. Afterwards . . . well, that's up to you. You'll be contacted nearer the time.'

She went over to the door and stood and looked at him. He was extremely controlled and his calm worried her. It wasn't a reaction she had expected. She had come prepared for violent argument – even violence. The latter had almost happened – earlier. Now he appeared to feel nothing. She didn't know if it was acceptance or not. It worried her that she had to go – not knowing – but a sixth sense warned her not to stay.

After she had gone he looked down at the paper which he still held in his hand. It was crumpled now and the writing looked even more distorted. Without a shadow of doubt it was Dee's writing. Without a shadow of doubt they intended murdering her if he didn't comply. He wished he could think clearly. He wished he could feel. His body was anaesthetized. He sat on in the room unaware of the gathering twilight that crept through the room like a dark mist.

It was a long time before Briony could pluck up the courage to open the door and go in to him. She went quietly over to the electric heater and the soft glow from it filled the room. The main light she left off. She sensed without touching him that he was cold. She had reacted that way, too. Her body had felt as if it had been rubbed with snow. She poured him some whisky and placed the glass in his hand. Dee's letter had fallen at the side of his chair and she made out the one word David in the glow from the heater. Sybil had given her no details of how the name had come to be written. The cassette – now the letter.

'David.'

He looked at her, barely aware of her.

'David – I didn't know it was going to be like this.'

He wished she would take her conscience away. She kept laying it at his feet like a burnt offering. An appeasement.

'Please.' She went and crouched on the chair opposite him, her legs drawn up under her.

'What do you want me to say to you?'

'That it's not my fault.'

He was silent.

117

She began to cry and her tears made him angry. 'Stop it – or get out. Get out anyway.'

She didn't move. 'I didn't know that Dee . . .'

'You knew she was being hurt. You heard the cassette.'

'I thought perhaps . . . frightened.'

'But now you know differently.' He looked at the whisky she had placed in his hand and drank a little of it. The liquid burned some life into him and like warmth after frostbite the pain came.

It was a long time before he was able to speak again. 'Why don't you go to bed? You can't do anything.'

'Neither can you.'

He wasn't so sure about that. 'Is Foster one of your people?'

'Who's Foster?'

'Then he isn't?'

'I don't know. Who is he?'

'Someone who might help.' He looked at the phone and remembered that it was bugged. Foster lived in Sloane Square. He decided to get the car out and drive there. Foster belonged to the Secret Intelligence Service. If the Group had Foster then they held the country in the palm of their hand.

Briony followed him to the door. 'You're going out?'

'Yes.'

'You know you'll be followed?'

'It's possible.'

'Be careful.'

'Is that a threat? Will you inform on me as soon as I've gone?'

She flinched as if he had struck her.

He apologized clumsily and then wondered at himself for apologizing. It would be perfectly natural for her to inform on him. That was her function . . . but she wouldn't.

The night was bright with neons that outdid the stars. A cold wind blew. The car started sluggishly and when the engine eventually began to turn one of Dee's gloves fell from the shelf under the dashboard and jammed against the gear lever. Like an omen, he thought. But he removed it and drove on.

There was a light in Foster's flat. He stopped the car and sat looking up at it. How would Foster react to what he had to say to him? 'You've been told to do *what*? Stop mixing your drinks, for Christ's sake!' He got out of the car and dodging the traffic made his way up to the steps of Foster's communal entrance. At the front door he stopped and turned to survey the street. A man and a girl, arms entwined, glanced casually at him and walked on. Two elderly women in identical coats of fawn suede walked briskly past. A man idled along as if he were myopic and careful of his footsteps, and at the corner he turned and retraced his steps. He glanced at David directly, but didn't stop. Several of the cars parked in the street were occupied as if the owners waited – or watched.

Foster's precise voice clicked through his head in imagined conversation. 'You were a fool to come to me, David. The Group is everything you have been told it is. Stop denying the power of something you don't want to believe in. Your disbelief won't diminish it. Your disbelief will kill Dee.'

When he returned to the flat Briony was sitting crouched in the chair again. She looked up at him, her eyes narrow with tiredness and trepidation.

'You haven't done anything – foolish?'

He dropped into the chair opposite. 'I haven't done anything at all.' The words were heavy with self-condemnation.

The only obvious person who knew nothing of the Group was the Prime Minister himself. Again he imagined the conversation. 'Don't attend the House on the first day of May, Prime Minister. I intend to bomb it. And you'd better pass that information on to the Leader of the Opposition, too. You're all in the target area.' 'Really, Berringer? How extraordinarily interesting! When did you see your psychiatrist last?'

If he approached the Prime Minister and gave him all the details

119

he knew and at the same time managed to persuade the PM of his sanity then the PM would act against the Group – insofar as he was able, for he too would be in the dark regarding the identity of the members. Dee's life held in balance against what the Prime Minister would see as the life of the nation would seem very unimportant.

For him the converse was true. If the nation wanted to run to its doom like a herd of Gadarene swine then he had no intention of throwing Dee into their path to stop them. But to encourage them over the brink . . . to carry cold-bloodedly the means of destruction . . . to maim and to kill . . .

He looked over at Briony. She was sitting back in her chair, her eyes closed, but she wasn't sleeping. Her memory of the bombing of the Silver Swan had sat on her shoulders like an old man of the sea and he had shown no sympathy.

And his own conscience if he went through with it . . .

If he went through with it and stayed in the House and let it happen to him, too . . .

But they needed him alive and if he didn't oblige . . .

Dee.

Briony opened her eyes and looked at him. She understood his torment. For him it would be worse than it was for her. She had moments of peace. He would have none.

'David.'

'Yes?'

'Nothing – just David.'

He understood that she understood. They sat on in silence as the night closed in.

TEN

Dee walked barefooted through the grass and the dog circling her, but not too close, could be heard though not seen. She knew that if she continued in the same direction the circles would become smaller. The knoll at the top of the hill was its limit of discretion. Once there it would show itself, creeping forward on its belly, daring her to go on. She had tried it twice. It had been trained to perfection.

She remembered Bunty, the fox-terrier she had been given on her eighth birthday. It had been a weakling puppy and her mother had fed it with milk from a pipette and let it lick malt from her finger. At night it had slept in a green cracker box padded with cotton-wool. Bunty had been trainable, too. It had sat up and begged for sweets. In its swagger years it had chased everything on wheels and been killed by a motorbike. She had loved it dearly.

The past kept coming back to her as if she were an old woman with heightened memories. The first day at infants school – small, wooden chairs in pastel shades of pink, blue and green – the smell of her red plastic pencil case when the sun warmed it. The scent of wet mint in the herb garden below the tennis court in the early evening. Adolescence. Her love for Marie on the French exchange holiday. Marie who was beautiful and had breasts. Steven, the tall thin boy-friend who wrote her poems and believed himself a reincarnation of Keates and she of Fanny Brawne.

David.

The dog was moving closer and she stopped. The heather scratched her feet and there were little globules of water on her insteps. As a child she had always liked to walk barefooted. Near the holiday cottage on the cliffs above a small Welsh cove there had been harebells, their petals crisp as paper. She used to lie amongst them so that they crisped about her face as the wind moved them.

Her mother's voice: 'Marriage built on affection and shared interests can be a good marriage.'

And later, her father's: 'If it's as good for you and David as it is for your mother and me then you're a very lucky couple.'

David.

Gentle love making – careful not to hurt. His voice warm against her face telling her it would get better for her. And it did.

Mack.

Her mind swerved away.

The cottage from here looked even smaller than it was. It crouched like a malignant dwarf in the middle of untamed fields. The barn with its rat colony had a padlocked door. The padlock wasn't necessary, nothing would have induced her into it. She stayed out of the cottage for long hours at a time. There was a sense of freedom in the open air. A limited freedom. She could lie back and watch the clouds move like mobile snow mountains. There were small creatures in the soil beneath her hands. Busy creatures. Helpless creatures. The air was full of changing scents. Wet soil. Wind blowing through clover.

She wondered when they would kill her.

She wondered what it would be like.

She had fallen off her bike when she was ten. It had been like falling through miles of blackness through a long thundering hole.

In school there had been a picture of an old man seated on a cloud. God. What they were asking David to do was just as impossible for him as it would be for the old man on the cloud to grow horns.

He wouldn't do it.

Not even for her.

When Mack had told her she had laughed in his face.

May Day. Nuts in May. Everyone crazily drunk. An all night party – once – rites of Spring – lots of sex for those that wanted it. Walking out of the party with David – she still a virgin and he knowing it. Marriage bells. Odd sound, marriage bells – insistent like gossiping neighbours – yak – yak – yak.

Love. What was love? Planting a bomb – blood – guts – pieces of flesh. For her?

She ran her hands down her thighs and knees. Her knees were cold. Colder than her hands. Her flesh. Their flesh. A plurality of flesh.

Mack, coming quietly up the hill behind her, said 'Dee.'

She became very still, cringing into herself, and then she turned to him slowly. 'Yes, what is it?'

'I've made a meal for us. Come and get it.'

The difference in her during the last few days appalled him. She seemed to have reverted – not only to childhood – but to another culture – another time. She didn't bother with her appearance at all. Her face now was smudged with mud where she had pushed back her hair with muddy hands. He had seen her several times lying in the grass as if it gave her some kind of elemental solace. On days when the wind blew she would stand in it, arms half-raised, eyes closed, as if it gave her some kind of benison. When the sun shone she smiled. When it rained he had seen her catch it on her tongue.

He sensed the darkness of the night frightened her, but didn't go in to console her. His presence, he knew, frightened her more. He didn't know what to do or what to say to give her reassurance. She

123

knew how her husband would react better than he did. She knew how the Group would react to David's failure – if he failed – even better than he did. She kept looking into his eyes and seeing death. He was learning to look away.

They walked down the hill together to the cottage. He had fried some bacon and mushrooms and the smell of them made a small knot of resistance form in her stomach. She sat at the table attempting to eat, knowing he would fuss if she didn't. Her feet were cold indoors and she rubbed one foot on the other. She hadn't slippers and didn't want to wear her shoes. These days he was full of small acts of kindness that disconcerted her. He fetched an old pullover from his bedroom and wrapped her feet in it. She didn't want to touch anything of his and slowly edged it away.

He noticed. 'Put your shoes on.'

'Later.'

'You'll catch cold.'

'It doesn't matter.'

'Are you going to eat any more of that?'

'I can't.'

'I wish you would ... All right ... don't worry.' He took the plate away.

He did everything in the cottage now. Cleaning and cooking as best he could.

He asked her if she wanted the television on.

She was indifferent. 'Please yourself.'

'There's ballet on Two. A play on Channel 4. A quiz on ITV. Which do you want?'

'None of them. Have what you want.'

He made no move to go over to the set. 'Will you talk to me?'

'What about?'

'About what frightens you.'

She made a small pushing gesture with her hands. 'Nothing frightens me. I don't know what you're talking about.'

124

'I would never hurt you – no matter what might happen – or not happen.'

She met his glance before he could look away. 'No,' she said, 'of course not.' There was no conviction in her voice.

He said after a long pause. 'I didn't see at the beginning how the road would go – I just saw the end of the road and the end seemed good.'

'But you still follow the road.'

'I take each corner as it comes. I think perhaps we're both imagining what isn't there.'

'You know what David has been asked to do.'

'I know now. I didn't at the commencement.'

'But if you had?'

He couldn't answer that. Not even to himself. How much evil was justified for the ultimate good?

She understood his silence. 'You see?'

'I don't think either of us sees. Not properly. Not yet.'

'But I do.' She left the table and went over to the fireplace. The fire was made but not lit. She looked down at the dull grate, shivering.

He noticed and flicked his lighter and held it to the paper. Flames curled softly. 'You'll soon be warm.'

'You shouldn't have lit it for me.'

'Why not? You're not going out again.'

'You mean you're forbidding me to go out again?'

'Don't be ridiculous.' He hesitated. 'Let me walk with you.'

'No . . . just me and the dog.' It was bitter.

He stood and watched her go. She was like a condemned prisoner walking within high boundary walls – only the walls here were fields of tall grass and a dog the jailer. The dog and himself.

He wondered what he would do if he were in David's position.

125

It would depend on the extent of his feeling for Dee.

That was the unknown factor.

An act of positive violence. Or failure to act followed by violence by default.

By this time tomorrow he would know. Tomorrow was May Day.

ELEVEN

The bomb, built by experts, lay snugly in the briefcase like a foetus in a womb. Major Anderson who was explaining the mechanism was a disposal expert with much skill but little imagination. He knew his bombs much as a plumber knew his S bends. The human element didn't concern him at all. Berringer had agreed to do it and any emotional reaction Berringer might have was the responsibility of the shrink merchants. He seemed calm enough. And the girl, too.

They were all in the study.

The girl was wearing a green polo-necked sweater and a black and green checked skirt. She looked as if she could do with a good night's sleep. Anderson wondered if she were having it off with Berringer.

Berringer himself didn't look too rested either, but he was listening to what Anderson was telling him with undivided attention. Which was just as well. This one was a beauty. It would go off with one hell of a pop.

'You understand how important it is to get the timing mechanism right?' He pointed out the controls once more. 'In every way it looks like a normal briefcase – the difference lies in these two locks here. This one on the right activates the bomb. One turn to the right in the quarter past three position. The locking movement that you have on your own briefcase.' He passed over the ordinary briefcase. 'Show me how you lock it.' He watched. 'Just so. You'll find the locking

127

movement just as easy as this one – but remember once you do it the bomb is activated.'

He pointed to the other key-hole. 'This is the timing device. It has been set for three-fifteen. The small notches indicate periods of quarter of an hour. They're not discernible unless you're looking for them, but they're clear enough when you are. If for any reason you want to delay the explosion by quarter of an hour you move this around, so. Now you show me three-thirty.'

David hesitated and the Major gave a snicker of laughter. 'It's not activated, man. It's perfectly safe. Go on – show me.'

David moved the lock and showed three-thirty.

'Splendid. Now three forty-five.'

David did so. The Major reminded him of a woodwork master who had taught him at school in the sane days of long ago when the smell in one's nostrils was woodshavings not cordite. He was finding it extremely difficult to believe in the bomb. His brain cells seemed to be closing down in mute refusal to accept that it was there and that all this was happening.

He glanced across at Briony. A suitcase containing a change of clothes had arrived for her the previous day. She looked different in them. Clean, collected, smooth. The untidy urchin quality that he had got used to had gone. He sensed a new hardness in her as if she were learning not to care. Conversation, never easy between them, was now almost nil. The night she had sat up with him had seemed to drain her of all feeling so that now she had nothing to offer. They were both arid, he thought. He felt nothing either. He didn't dare feel anything.

The Major put him through the motions again and got him to re-time the explosion for a quarter past three. 'Once you turn the keyhole here and activate the bomb, you will have a quarter of an hour to leave the House. In order to make your exit seem natural Pruet will come up to you at three o'clock with a note. You will leave with him.'

Pruet? So Pruet was one of them, too? Or perhaps Pruet was just being used. Well, at least Pruet wouldn't die, that would be one off his conscience.

'Are you going to the House in your own car?'

'Yes. Is there any reason why I shouldn't?'

'No. Leave the briefcase on the floor – not on the seat. If it got jerked off the seat the timing mechanism might alter fractionally. Try to drive smoothly. Would you like me to drive you?'

'No. I'm perfectly capable of driving myself.'

And he was, he realized, perfectly capable. Not a tremor of nerves.

'Well, good-luck.' The Major held out his hand and David took it. They shook hands formally. The Atkinson woman had shaken his hand, too. They were a formal lot, the Group. Murder most civilized.

There were a few minutes before he need leave for the House. He went up to the bathroom, relieved himself, and then he washed his hands with some of Dee's yellow soap. He looked at his face in the mirror. If the Hyde in his nature had taken over it didn't show.

It would be very easy to stay in the bathroom now. To shave again. Perhaps to bath. To lie back in the water and let the time tick by. He took a small scissors from the drugs cabinet and cut his fingernails.

Dee's hand. Dee's incapable of writing hand. Had it been lighted matches under her fingernails? Or had they removed the fingernails one by one?

He put the scissors in the cabinet and went down the stairs. He couldn't delay any longer. He would have to go now. He picked up the briefcase. It was considerably heavier than his own. That was the only external difference.

Briony was waiting in the hall. She was standing near a Turner reproduction that showed calm green fields. The green was the same green as her pullover. He wished that she was still wearing that sleeveless red thing. Her arms had looked like sticks in it but somehow it suited her better. Red for revolution. Red for blood. He blanked the thought and let it trickle away from his mind.

She came towards him, her arm out, and for a moment he thought she was going to shake hands, too. The Group gesture. Instead, carefully so as not to touch the briefcase she put her arm around his neck and drew his face down to hers. The kiss was brief and unexpected and was over before he knew it.

She stood back and looked at him.

He hoped to God she wasn't going to wish him good-luck.

She said nothing and neither did he. She opened the door for him and he went out without a backward glance.

The sun had been on the car all the morning and the interior smelt of warm leather. He placed the briefcase on the floor as instructed and then, almost in a ritual gesture, looked for and found Dee's glove. He laid it carefully on the briefcase. Justification? He didn't know. It seemed the right thing to do.

The traffic was no easier and no more difficult than usual. He drove with his usual care, neither more nor less. If a careless bus should decide to mangle him – well, that was up to the bus. A different lot of people would die. It was Russian roulette with a bullet in every chamber.

London in the Spring. It was an incredibly nice day. He hadn't noticed before how many people grew flowers in window-boxes. He hadn't done anything about Dee's window-boxes since she had gone. He had forgotten all about it. Not surprisingly. When she came back he would help her dig it out and re-stock it. She liked flowers. Usually the flat was filled with flowers. She was fond of colour and interesting textures. She had an eye for clothes and chose them well. He liked to lie in bed and watch her dressing. Pants and bra with lace. Soft materials that seemed to sigh against her skin as she pulled them on. She liked him to brush her hair. She would toss the brush over to him and he would get her to sit on the edge of the bed. Sometimes half-dressed he would pull her back into bed with him. She had been slow to arouse in the early days, but as time had gone on . . . until that period with Mackilroy . . .

A car horn blared and he took swift avoiding action. The glove on the briefcase slid onto the floor.

He wondered how long her hand would take to heal. She had always been proud of her fingernails. She had beautiful hands and she took great care of them. She was fastidious in every way – in her person – in her clothes – and in the way she ran the flat. She was a charming hostess and a wonderful cook.

> *She was becoming words in his mind.*
> *He daren't lose the reality of her.*
> *She had to be more than words.*
> *If she were words only he couldn't go on.*

He reached over and picked up the glove and began finding her again in the feel of it.

The Palace of Westminster was bathed in warm ochre sunlight. It was on such a day that he had first taken his seat. He remembered how he had signed the roll and made his oath of affirmation to the Crown. He had been one of the youngest MPs there. Raw. Naive. Hopeful. As proud as a peacock with two tails. The memory had come unbidden and he tried to kick it away.

He parked the car and leaned over to pick up the briefcase. Dee's glove was in his left hand and he picked up the briefcase with his right. The unaccustomed weight of the case seemed to equal the weight of his spirits. His footsteps were slow as he left the car. He stood for a few minutes and listened to the river noises. 'Sweet Thames run softly till I end my song.' He was back at school. Till I end my song. The smell of ink. It had been ink in those days. Fountain pens – not inkwells. He had copied out the poem. Why? He couldn't remember why. 'Till I end my song.' Whose song would he end today? – Not Dee's song. Please God – if you exist out there somewhere – let her go on singing. Let her be strong again. Let her be well. Let her live.

Please God.

It was a blasphemy.

This thing in his hand was a blasphemy.

To call on God was blasphemy with this thing in his hand.

A familiar voice said behind him, 'Lingering in the Spring sunshine, Berringer? I know how you feel. It's a day for the links. Do you play much these days?'

Dan Miller, present Minister of Agriculture, wore gold-framed glasses which he seemed to use more for gesticulating with than to aid his vision. He pushed them low on his nose now and looked at David over them.

'Not a lot.' They fell into step, walking slowly. Miller began talking about his son who had had a double first at university. 'He wants to travel. Not settle down yet. He came home for the weekend and we played nine holes. I can't manage much more than that. Out of practice, I suppose. It's all this sitting around. He's bringing his girl friend to the visitor's gallery this afternoon.'

David's hand tightened on Dee's glove.

Miller, who never bothered whether he was answered or not, went on, 'She's more interested in parliamentary affairs than Bobby ever was. Unless she's just being nice to the old man – maybe that's it. She's at the LSE. Pretty kid – fair hair – nice legs. You've no youngsters yet, have you, Berringer?'

'No.'

'Well, it's a strange old world to bring them into – but I suppose it always was in one way or another. I'm not happy about the defence cuts, but you've heard all that. You know my views. Are you staying on for the debate on further education at the end of the afternoon?'

'I'm not sure.'

132

Miller looked at him with a degree of surprise. Berringer usually sat in on everything. He was one of the keenest members in the House. Rumour had it that his wife had upped and offed and that he was taking it hard. It certainly looked that way. The man looked ill. He had come a long way in his political career and he had come a long way fast. He was well liked which, under the circumstances, was unusual. Success wasn't a likeable quality. It would be a pity if his marriage broke up when he was reaching the peak. He was Prime Minister material. The only time he had ever put a foot wrong was when he had given that paranoid broadcast and he had even made that sound credible. He wondered what had possessed him.

A sudden memory struck him. 'Do you remember your first day, Berringer. You wanted to know what the tape was for on your peg in the cloakroom and when I told you it was for hanging your sword on you thought I was taking the mickey.' He chuckled. 'Archaic ritual and codswallop, but I wouldn't have it different.'

It was time for the Speaker's Procession through the central lobby and the Members' lobby en route for the Chamber. The police officers standing guard along the way passed on the command: 'Hats off Strangers!'

David glimpsed the startled face of a young girl as she heard the words and then saw her biting back a smile. The gallery would be opened to the public only after the procession had entered the Chamber and prayers had been said.

Prayers.

Eyes to the wall.

A jumble of often repeated words that didn't normally make any more impact on him than a buzzing of bees. Now he had to steel himself not to listen or think.

The House was full. The Gallery was crowded. He tried to see Miller's son and the girl friend but couldn't distinguish them from a blur of faces. It was as well. To survive this he had to try to see it as a stage-set. In the early days he had seen it that way. Up to the time of his maiden speech he had been a member of the audience. The speech had been his first walking-on part. And then the drama had got him. He had learnt to make up for the part – to use psychological high-lighting. Pitch of voice. Gesture. But there had always been basic honesty. No true actor or politician had a cat's chance in hell without that.

The Speaker was on his feet going through the preliminary announcements very rapidly, passing minor unopposed bills with the words, 'The ayes have it, the ayes have it.' All this was routine.

David sat back and it washed around him like waves on a rocky beach. He tried to hold on to the imagery of the sea. Dee with him at Polperro the summer before they married. They had taken a boat out and Dee had tried to row it. She had nearly lost an oar. He tried to see her as she had been then, but her face was a mist in his mind and he couldn't see a single feature.

He put the briefcase under the bench by his feet.

Question Time had started. Notice of questions had to be given two days in advance so that the relevant information could be on hand for the Minister concerned. No question today concerned his department. He wondered to what extent that had been arranged or was it coincidence? Not coincidence, he decided. They wouldn't take that kind of risk.

The Minister of Health was on his feet. He had the skill and energy of a squash player smashing back the criticism so that it bounced in a favourable direction.

The Life Force. Shaw had said a lot about that. Don Juan in Hell.

There had been a drowned man on the beach at Polperro. The tide had carried him up against the rocks. His half naked body had been twined with sea-weed and was grey and swollen. He had managed to turn Dee away before she saw him. He still couldn't see Dee. The drowned man's face was very clear. The flesh had started to pull away around his eyes and his mouth was purple and slack. Death by seawater. Slow. The saliva was rising in his throat and he

134

felt sick. He moved his heel back and felt the briefcase.

The Prime Minister and the Leader of the Opposition had started a slanging match. Valid arguments on both sides. Both getting heated but trying not to show it. A rustle of unrest amongst members. Anger, for the most part simulated, growling up to the surface.

The tempo was quickening and excitement in the gallery could be felt like an electric current. This was what they had come to see. Like spectators at a race meeting watching the jockeying for position – looking to see if the spurs drew blood – they arched forward in expectancy. a beam of sunlight highlighted a blonde head.

Dan Miller, seated on his left, said 'That's her. Enjoying every minute of it. Odd sort of birthday treat, but this is what she wanted.'

'Birthday?' It came out normally.

'Yes. Today. Nineteen.'

'Oh.'

'What's the matter?'

'Matter?'

'You've got the shakes. Night out last night?'

David placed his hand carefully on his knees until he could feel the bones. The tremor extended up his arms. He hadn't been aware of it.

'Yes, a night out.'

He couldn't do it. In five minutes' time he would have to activate a bomb that would kill amongst others a nineteen-year-old girl. He tried to assess her chances of escape. The bomb that had failed to kill Hitler had had the blast deflected by the table. The blast here would be better deflected if the bomb were placed under the clerks' table that stood in front of the Speaker's dais, but he couldn't deliberately pick up the briefcase, go forward from his bench, and place it there. And even if he could by what right could he choose to mete out certain death to the men who sat at it? The bomb was

135

intended for the leading parliamentarians on both sides of the House. If the leaders weren't killed today then the Group no doubt would dispatch them with all speed in some seeming accident tomorrow. Nothing would be left to chance.

Those who remained in the House after he left it would be ignorant of the Group. If he made the motions of activating it and then returned and revealed the conspiracy he would be listened to and something would be done.

But would he be listened to?

And if something were done it wouldn't be done quickly enough to save Dee.

The Prime Minister was parrying a question about the rising cost of living. Percentages were being quoted. It was two fifty-seven.

His mind wasn't functioning. They were wasting precious moments with trivia. He wanted to get up and yell at them to shut up – to shut up and get out. Without being aware of it he was muttering the words between his teeth. Miller, thinking he was having a go at the opposition, grinned and took it up louder, 'Shut up and get out!'

The Prime Minister looked over in their direction; amusement gleamed temporarily before the mask of gravity was resumed.

Pruet said quietly, 'Admiral Jackson is waiting by your car. He wants to see you now – urgently.'

David said, 'Yes.'

He bent down to retrieve the briefcase. Jackson and his henchmen could burn in hell. They had asked the impossible of him.

The briefcase was on his knee.

He looked up at gallery to see if he could see the blonde head, but the beam of sunlight had gone.

Pruet said, 'I think this is yours, sir. I think you must have dropped it.'

It was Dee's glove. Small, lightly perfumed. Dee's hand. The scream on the cassette. The maimed appeal . . . David.

136

The Chamber seemed to close in on him, like a vast echoing cavern in which sea-voices surged and retreated and then surged again. And then clearly he saw Dee's face – her eyes, dark and questioning – her mouth unsmiling.

Pruet held it out, waiting for him to take it. Instead he turned the activating switch on the bomb one quarter turn to the right.

Pruet exhaled his breath quietly. 'Leave it on the bench, sir. You'll be returning later.' This was for the benefit of anyone listening who might survive.

David said, 'Yes,' and began walking away. He felt as if he pushed through solid air that formed in his lungs like crepe. When he got out in the sunlight he didn't at first know where he was. It was Pruet who took him by the arm and guided him to the car.

Admiral Jackson was seated at the wheel. 'Give me the keys, Berringer. I'll drive.' He looked at Pruet and Pruet nodded. 'The car keys, Berringer. Where do you keep them?'

David looked at him dazed, the words not registering.

Pruet said, 'In your jacket pocket – may I look?' He put his hand in and found them. He handed them over.

The Admiral was holding open the door on the passenger side. 'Get in, David . . . Pruet will stay around and report later.' It was like severing an umbilical cord, Jackson thought. Berringer was now a separate entity from the Mother of Parliaments and the swift piece of surgery had put him in a state of shock. It was a pity it had to be such a bloody business. He asked him how he felt.

He didn't answer. He had an odd subterranean feeling as if he burrowed through a long grey tunnel while above him the noise of life went on.

Jackson said, 'I'll drive you over to your flat and stay with you there for a while. You'll have to prepare yourself for a television appearance this evening. There will have to be an explanation as to why you left the House this afternoon. I'll give you details of that later and gen you up with what you have to say. The take-over

137

should be painless and complete by the end of the week. Don't worry about any evidence – what's left of the briefcase you carried in will be taken care of.'

The mid-afternoon traffic wasn't heavy and Jackson drove fairly fast. He half expected David to command him to turn the car around and go back and the greater the distance he put behind him the better.

David said, 'In about four minutes.'

'Yes. The sound may not carry this far.'

'It's too late to prevent.'

Jackson looked sideways at him. 'It was too late the moment you activated it.'

'You've turned me into a murderer.'

'We all have freedom of choice.'

'Oh yes,' David said, 'we all have freedom of choice.' Hate was making the tunnel less grey. It was a positive emotion. This vicious, sadistic bastard seated at his side should be smashed through the windscreen.

Jackson spoke smoothly, 'You did it for your wife. Hang on to that and you'll find it more bearable.'

'When do I see her?'

'Quite soon if you act with commonsense.'

'Commonsense? By God – commonsense!' Laughter bubbled in his throat like bitter water. He thought, I'm as mad as the rest of them. Initiated into their mad bloody clan.

In less than two minutes . . .

He began counting his heartbeats . . .

In less than one minute . . .

A matter of seconds now . . .

The throb in his head was like a sledge hammer.

Jackson turned the car into the quiet tree-lined Kensington road and drew up near the flat.

And then the bomb went off.

The whole street seemed to contract and then to swell with a hidden force that blew out doors and windows and hurled debris into the sky. A For Sale sign from across the road splintered against the car bonnet and metal railings billowed outwards like hot plastic. The reverberations died away into total silence.

It was several minutes before David understood what had happened. Admiral Jackson was the first to put it into words. His face was grey. 'So you switched the briefcases and murdered Briony. Not clever of you, Berringer – not clever at all.'

David got out of the car and began walking towards the blackened doorway. He walked very slowly and very steadily. He didn't know that there were tears on his cheeks. He didn't know that he was calling her name – softly – quietly.

Briony.

Someone put a hand on his arm and tried to stop him going into the flat, but he shook it off. He stood in the shattered hallway and looked around him. The thick cloud of dust was in his eyes and in his mouth so that he choked and retched.

That she had switched the briefcases deliberately he had no doubt.

She had done this for him.

TWELVE

Mack, crouching over the transmitter in the barn, heard the news of the Kensington bomb and knew that for him the road had come to an abrupt and unexpected end. His contact gave him the news unemotionally. Briony was the only casualty and wasn't expected to survive. The other residents of the adjoining flats were out at the time of the explosion. Berringer would neither admit nor deny that he had picked up the wrong briefcase intentionally. It was he who had found Briony at the bottom of the back staircase leading to the basement flat. She hadn't been pretty to look at and he had gone over to the garden wall and been sick. They hadn't been able to get a word out of him since. Now that a balls-up had been made of the original plan, his contact went on, the alternative would be put in action. Commander Stringer would be sent out to the cottage and Mackilroy was to hand over to him. Did he understand?

Mack answered clearly that he did.

And the conversation ended.

He sat back on the straw and noticed a rat skittering into a corner. Up to now results had been obtained by make-believe. All the violence had been pseudo-violence. From now on it would be different. Had Berringer refused to activate the bomb in the House of Commons, Dee might still have stood a chance of survival. By exploding it in the flat with the intention of killing Briony he had signed Dee's death warrant. It was now a matter of hours.

141

He went into the fields and found her near the knoll of trees. The dog close, but not too close, lay panting in the shade. The afternoon was warm and the air was filled with the soft humming of gnats. She sat with her arms entwined around her knees and there were grass stains on her skirt.

He said abruptly, 'You were right. He didn't do it.'

He couldn't understand her calmness, her complete lack of curiosity as three-fifteen had come and gone. He had invited her to come into the barn with him and listen to the news as it came through, perhaps in the event it was just as well she didn't.

She said, 'No – how could he?'

'If I had been in his shoes, I would have done it for you.'

'That's easy to say. Perhaps you find killing easy. He doesn't.'

'He had no qualms about Briony.' He told her about the Kensington bomb.

For the first time her eyes registered surprise, but she said nothing.

He sat down on the grass beside her. One person, he thought. Just one person. A tired face. Sunshine on her uncombed hair. Was that how things ended? Sabotage by one person. Years of commitment falling away into nothing. He had been a fool to accept the assignment. Or had he accepted it knowing with one small part of his mind that it would end this way and that he would have to be here?

'How much does David mean to you, Dee?'

The question took her by surprise and she didn't know how to answer. The fact that he hadn't activated the bomb put her second in his order of priorities. She didn't resent it. He just hadn't believed that they would harm her. Their pressure hadn't been strong enough. Basically good himself, he hadn't believed in the evil of others. He didn't understand. When he finally did understand it would be too late.

She had been frightened for a long time now. After a while even fear lost its edge.

He repeated the question, 'How much does David mean to you?'

'Why?'

'I was wondering how you would feel if you didn't see him again?'

'Under the circumstances I thought he would do the feeling – not me.'

'What do you mean?' But he understood her.

'You know what I mean. When is it going to happen?' She turned and looked at him, her eyes dark with hopelessness.

'It's not going to happen. They're sending out a man called Stringer who is supposed to take over from me. When he gets here we'll be gone.'

'Gone where?'

Christ alone knew, he thought. The only safe bolt hole he knew was Mason's farm in the Cotswolds. They had gone on a flying course together. Mason had a light aircraft used for crop spraying. Mason would put them up for the night and let them borrow the plane for a flip tomorrow if he made it sound casual enough. The plane had enough fuel capacity to take them to France and France would do for a start.

He thought he had better give it to her a little at a time. 'We'll spend tonight at a friend's place – a farm near Stroud. He's never heard of the Group. His only politics are in the pages of the *Farmers' Weekly*. I can't think of anyone safer to go to.'

She looked at him distrustfully. Not sure of the offer of the open door and what lay beyond it.

He understood that, too. Fear that built up slowly took a long while to go. The only way to get her to move was not to pull any punches. Her fear had to be channelled in the right direction. 'Stringer is a Commander in a specially trained combat unit. He isn't coming here to let a rat loose on your bed – or to get you to write with your left hand. He means to harm you. I didn't think when I started this that you'd be hurt. But you are going to be if you don't come away with me now. I don't know how far we'll get – or what will happen. But whatever happens will happen to the two of us. Do you understand me?'

A jailer turned liberator. It wasn't easy to understand, still less easy to believe, but the menace of the other man outweighed her doubts about Mack, there seemed nothing else to do but to accompany him.

He reached out his hand to pull her to her feet, but she refused to touch it and got up slowly.

When they were in the cottage he found it difficult to hurry her. The slow tempo of her way of life since the Admiral's visit had become the sluggishness of despair and she couldn't be forced back to normality by anything he might say or do. He did the packing for the two of them, not that there was much to pack. He always carried his passport in his wallet. She wouldn't have hers, but they'd cross that bridge when they came to it. He had enough loose cash to get by for a while.

He went into the bedroom to see what she was doing and saw that she was seated at the dressing-table and was making up her face. It was something she hadn't bothered to do for a long time. He held back his impatience, watching her. The blue shadow on her lids was almost the same colour as the natural shadows under her eyes. She worked in blusher high on her cheekbones and it looked startling against her natural pallor. She tried to rub it away again. Her hair was neat now, combed back off her forehead.

She smiled wryly at her image. 'The American way of death.'

'What?'

'In America the corpses are made up before they're encapsulated in ice.'

'Shut up!'

The fur wrap she had arrived in was draped over the end of the bed. He threw it over at her. 'Take that with you. You might need it later.'

144

'And my evening gown – are we going to a ball?' It was ironic.

'No. I don't think you'll be needing that for a while.'

The possibility that his actions would be anticipated by Jackson worried him. Jackson's reflective look during his last visit hadn't been lost to him. Jackson regarded him as an unknown quantity. A dedicated Group member but with an emotional commitment. It was the fact of his emotional commitment that had made them release him from the assignment. Under different conditions he would have been ordered to see the assignment through. He wondered how he would have acted if it had been anyone else. To kill was the ultimate act of dedication. They had asked it of Berringer. That they would ask it of him had never seriously occurred to him. A revolutionary spirit was one thing, cold-blooded murder another. He still believed in the aims of the Group, but the means lay like a sickness in his stomach. His action now would be regarded as weakness. A chain was as strong as its weakest link and he would be cut out of the chain. By leaving the cottage now with Dee he would be turning his back on a way of life that he had believed both possible and desirable. Chauvinism according to the dictionary definition was political fanaticism. All right – so he was a fanatic. He had believed that Britain needed a military backbone so that she could stand up against the infiltration of Marxism and hit back hard. He had believed in non-party government conducted by the best brains in the country. Intellectual éliteism. If he left the cottage now – on his own – and returned to London that way of life would still be possible in the foreseeable future. He wanted it. It was right.

But the means were wrong.

By leaving now with Dee he would be going into voluntary exile – or worse.

She, too, had been thinking. 'You asked me how I would feel if I didn't see David again – what did you mean?'

'I meant that you had to get away.'

'But for how long?'

'I don't know. What I do know is that if we don't leave here quickly we might not have the chance to leave at all.'

· Her mind was still too bludgeoned by events to assess the new twist to the situation. 'Why won't you drive me back to London – to David – now?'

He was angry with her for not understanding. 'We wouldn't get anywhere near David. I don't know what will happen in the future, but if you don't do as I tell you now you won't be around in the future to find out.'

When they went out to the van he told her to sit in the back out of sight. It didn't help their relationship, but it would be safer for her if an attempt were made to stop the van. Rough justice on the spot wouldn't be beyond the scope of the Group's hit men. He had seen it happen in Ireland. A different cause, similar methods. At least the Group didn't lay any claim on God.

She sat on the long narrow bunk and looked out through the van's back window. The May sun streamed over the young green fields in great swathes of yellow. Lambs almost as big as the ewes butted their mother's teats. It was all so normal. A pretty English day drawing towards evening. He was keeping to the minor roads and the half-awake village streets seemed to shudder their disapproval as the van rumbled through. David had wanted to buy a cottage they had seen in Dorset, but she hadn't been keen. The roses around the door, lavender in the garden, antidote to daily stress didn't appeal to her. A cottage like that needed children. The evenings with just the two of them would have palled into boredom. She tried to see David with the deeper part of her mind but there had been too much trauma. She was like a patient slowly returning to consciousness after an operation. She had expected to die under the knife and hadn't. Impressions of life like pictures on a screen passed before her. She was expected to accept the incredible. David and a bomb. The kindly, conventional, dedicated Minister of the Crown being forced to destroy everything he believed in. Only he hadn't. He had destroyed the girl instead. Why? Why kill Briony? Perhaps he hadn't meant it to happen. Surely he couldn't have meant it to happen. They didn't say she was dead. Dying. But that was worse . . .

And what would they do to David? The reprisal of her own death had been like a dark smoke-screen blotting everything else out – she hadn't thought about the consequences of his action beyond that.

She turned and looked at Mack. He was concentrating wholly on the driving, hunched a little over the wheel. They hadn't spoken for a long while.

'What will they do to David?'

He wondered why she had been such a long time asking it, but recognized the depth of her anxiety now that the facts were finally getting through to her.

He answered as honestly as he could. 'Probably nothing. They'll examine his reasons and then decide whether he's still usable or not.'

'Usable?' It was an odd word.

'They won't pin any medals on him for what he's done, but he's still their original choice. They might still be able to force him into the role they intended for him. I don't know.'

'They won't . . . kill . . . him?' The word was hard to say.

'No. I honestly believe they won't.' He thought: At least, not yet. But kept the thought to himself. 'They asked too much of him too soon. It was misjudgment on their part. They'll reassess his potential in the light of what they know.' It sounded cold-blooded, but he hoped it reassured her.

There was a herd of cows at the next crossroads and he was forced to bring the van to a slow crawl. There was a car parked on the road to the left with a man sitting in it. It was an odd place to park a car. There were no houses in the immediate vicinity. The cows were effectively blocking both his own exit and the other

147

driver's. Had the other driver wanted to drive on he could have got through a couple of minutes earlier. He was definitely parked – not blocked. He told Dee to lie on the floor of the van and cover herself with the bunk cushions.

'What?' She still wasn't alert.

'The van isn't bullet-proof. Do as I say and lie down.'

He glanced back over his shoulder to satisfy himself that she did so. The man in the car was a stranger to him. He had aquiline features and thin grey hair cropped short. The cross-roads could be reached from other minor roads and was a good point of interception. He might have done better to have risked the major roads, but it was too late to have second thoughts about it now. He was probably doing everything he was expected to do. If he were the pursuer and not the pursued he would have tailed the van unobtrusively, ascertained its general direction, looked for short-cuts and a likely place for a showdown. Such as here. A herd of cows was an unforseen complication. If the cows took the right fork at the cross-roads then the car would converge on the van. If they took the left fork, the van would get through. They were being herded by a young girl in a white mackintosh. He leaned out of the van and asked her which way she was taking them. She answered in thick Gloucestershire that they were on their way to the Maltings farm down yonder in Little Silbury. He couldn't see the signboard from where he sat, but she was indicating the right fork. He jumped out of the van and gave her a fiver. 'Take them the other way.'

She fingered the note, too astonished to speak.

'Please. It's a joke on a friend of mine over there.'

She looked at the other car and a slow grin spread over her face. He winked at her and she winked back.

'Hup – hup – there Patsy. Hup – hup – Lizzie . . .' She beat her stick against her wellingtons and ran up to the leading cows. They didn't want to be turned away from the familiar route and she was

148

having difficulty in forcing them. He sat back in the van tapping his fingers impatiently on the wheel. The first two were taking the left fork. The man in the car tried to edge through them but the third and fourth effectively blocked the road. Mack began to drive the van forward and the bonnet met the rump of a cow that had stopped to crop the grass verge. Frightened, it tried to mount the cow in front of it, and then they all began to run, some to the right and some to the left. The road ahead was clear. He forced the accelerator down hard.

He drove the van dangerously for the next few miles and then, satisfied that the road behind was clear, told Dee that she could sit up again.

It had been a rough ride lying on the floor and she was shaken and bruised. 'What was it?'

'A parked car. I didn't like the look of it.'

'But surely no-one would know we'd left the cottage.'

'They would have anticipated the possibility.'

'You mean, they're not sure of you?'

'Good girl, you're coming alive.' He looked at her over his shoulder and gave her a brief smile.

He sensed that though she was still not sure of him either, some of her fear of him was going.

She tried exploring a situation she still didn't fully understand. 'You believed in the Group – what they stood for?'

'Yes.'

'But not any more?'

'Yes, I still believe in them. I hope they succeed.'

'Then why are you taking me away now?'

'I've told you – I don't want you hurt.'

'Killed.'

He didn't answer.

'That man in the car – if he had been one of them – what would he have done to you?'

149

'That would depend on his orders and his ability to carry them out.'

'Would he have murdered the two of us?'

'He might have tried.'

'And yet you still believe in a Group – a system – or whatever you want to call it that employs a bunch of murdering thugs.'

'All governments employ hit men to do their dirty work for them.'

'And you condone it?'

'Of course not, but I'm a realist.'

'Then why don't you turn the van round now and give me up to the man at the cross-roads?'

Why indeed? Because he had loved her once – perhaps still did, but in a different way. The situation they had been forced to put up with had turned them into two different people. The woman he had known on the Scottish holiday wasn't the woman he knew now. His feeling for her now was a caring one – as if she were a child – or very old.

'Why?' She was demanding an answer.

'Because you are you and I am myself.' Beyond that he couldn't go.

When they reached the woods near Mason's farm and he turned the van into them and drove it down a track dark with trees some of her fear returned.

'Why have you brought me here?'

He explained patiently that he had brought the van there because the quicker it was ditched and they were out of it the better.

'Tim Mason's farm is about a quarter of a mile away at the other side of the woods and over a couple of fields. We'll tell him we've had clutch trouble and ask him to put us up for the night.'

She got out of the van and her shoes crunched on pine cones. Birds rustled in the depths of the trees and a small wind blew. If he were going to kill her he would kill her now. The elaborate charade would end here in a setting of sepulchral pines with the night coming on. She leaned against the van shivering.

He guessed her thoughts and felt a pain deep in his gut. 'Dee, don't be a fool.'

She didn't pretend to misunderstand. 'But how am I to know?'

'Look at me.' He went over and gently took her chin in the fingers of his right hand. She cringed away like a frightened animal and then was still, allowing his hand to stay there. Softly, carefully, he moved his other hand over and rubbed his thumb gently against her cheek. She was breathing very quickly and then gradually she breathed more normally. Her eyes that had seemed to be drowning in a slow death under his gaze slowly focused and she was calm.

'Mack, I'm sorry.' There were tears in her voice.

'So am I – that you felt that way – that I made you feel that way.'

He heard a car passing the woods entrance. It stopped – reversed – and the engine was switched off. He drew her back into the bushes. The van was obscured from the road by trees. A twig snapped as someone approached. Silence, then a hissing as the man relieved himself against a clump of bracken. More twigs cracking as the man returned to the road. The car engine starting up and the drone off into silence.

Dee said, 'Not the man at the cross-roads.'

'No – but it might have been.'

She brushed leaves off her skirt. 'We can't keep on running. What are we going to do?'

'We can keep running and we shall keep running – what the hell else can we do?'

'But running where?'

They began walking down the path through the trees and he told her about the aircraft. 'We both trained for our pilot's licences at the same flying club. He uses his plane for crop spraying. It's a two-seater and I've flown it several times.'

She halted, 'But for God's sake – fly it where?'

151

He had been thinking about it. There was a flying club in Normandy that he had landed at a couple of times. He told her France.

'You mean you're going to steal his aeroplane?'

'Yes. Temporarily. Our need is greater than his.'

She looked at him as if he were going out of his mind. 'I don't believe it.'

'Then you'd better start believing it. There's been Group infiltration into the whole fabric of the country for a long time now. I have to get you out of it.'

'But what about David?'

'David would want you to keep alive. Your best chance of keeping alive is by leaving the country.'

The trees were casting long shadows over the path; their roots, here and there above the surface like entwined snakes, made walking difficult. She had had no idea that the ramifications of the Group had spread so subtly and so far. Like the forest they were all around, dark, menacing and closing in.

'What are you going to tell your friend about us?'

He wondered if he dared suggest it. 'I haven't seen him for over a year. If I told him you were my wife, he would believe me.'

She stiffened. 'But is that necessary?'

'No, but I think I might be able to take better care of you if we spend the night together. His place is large and rambling. He would happily bed us down in one room, married or not, but I don't think Peggy would.'

'Peggy?'

'His wife.'

She was silent, turning it over in her mind. 'You think that even in his place an attempt might be made to – to get me?'

He noticed that she didn't use the word kill, though the implication was there. 'I think you're safer there than anywhere else, but I want to be around.'

152

'Won't they recognize me as David's wife?' She had been photographed at several functions with David, smiling her stretched, achingly bored smile for the benefit of the cameras.

He thought it extremely unlikely. In her black jersey and grass-stained skirt she looked more like someone on the run from an orphanage than the wife of a Cabinet Minister.

'It will be a very long shot if they do. Our luck has held until now.' It was unlucky, he thought, to talk about luck, but her morale needed boosting. She would need to meet the Masons calmly. She would need to talk and smile as if the occasion were a normal one. He asked her if she would like to sit and rest for a while until she felt more prepared.

'I could sit forever and not be prepared. My life is turning inside out. But I'll do my best.'

The farmhouse was Queen Anne and the gables caught the last glare of the dying sun. Restored with love and expertise it lay in a hollow in the hills like a beautiful relic of a more gracious age hidden from the modern world. The farm buildings, including the hangar, were new and built of local stone.

The Masons, both in their early forties, seemed as much part of the place as the surrounding hills. Even Dee in her highly nervous state was aware of an aura of timelessness about them. Their ancestors, she guessed, had tilled these same fields.

Their greeting, after initial surprise quickly suppressed, was tinged with old-world charm. They gave the impression that it was perfectly natural for a couple of guests to turn up out of the blue and spend the night at the farm. Mack's elaborate explanation about failure to get the car towed to the nearest garage was dismissed as a nonsensical idea anyway. Still more nonsensical to try to get accommodation at the local inn. It was a dreadful place, Peggy said. She was delighted to see Mack again and especially delighted to meet his wife. Why hadn't she and Tim been told that he had married? He must tell them all about it as they sat down to the

153

evening meal. They hadn't eaten, she hoped?

Mack said, no, they hadn't eaten. He was ravenously hungry. The meal of home-cured ham and salad followed by fresh fruit and cream, and a bland cheese made in their own dairy was excellent. He wished that Dee would do more than pick at it. She was trying hard to adapt to a normal way of life again and was even managing to converse a little. The story of their 'marriage' she left to him. He glossed over it as best he could. Tim looked at him with amused scepticism barely veiled. Peggy, he hoped, would misinterpret her husband's expression. Or, perhaps, she hadn't noticed.

After the meal they went into the sitting-room and Dee steeled herself to endure a conversation that ground on and on. Tim, slight of build, and with curly ginger hair turning grey, looked like a contented monkey comfortably settling into the chair for a night of reminiscences with Mack. He was obviously pleased to see him.

Mack steered the conversation to flying and the relative merits of the Cessna One Fifty and the Piper Cherokee. Tim said he still had the Rallye Commodore and while she remained airworthy he intended keeping her. He turned and smiled at Dee, 'It's a small French plane, adapted for crop spraying. Have you ever been in a two-seater?'

'No.'

'Then you don't know what flying is.'

Mack took it up quickly. 'That's what I tell her. I shall have to get in touch with the garage tomorrow morning, but before I do perhaps I could take Dee up for a flip?'

Peggy protested that the plane was filthy. 'It works for its living like the rest of the farm machinery.'

Her husband said, 'Since when did that ever stop you going up in her? She does a good job of spraying and a good job of flying.' He addressed Dee again. 'Mack's a good pilot. We both got our PPL under the same instructor. Does flying appeal to you?'

154

Peggy answered before she could. 'What appeals to Dee at this particular moment is a good night's sleep.' She smiled at her. 'Come and I'll show you the guest room.'

When Mack eventually went upstairs Dee was in bed. He looked at her with a degree of amusement. 'I suppose Peggy gave you that hideous nylon nightdress?'

'Yes.'

'Is that adjoining room a bathroom?'

'Yes.'

'Has it a separate exit?'

'There's another door. I tried it before I bathed. It's locked.'

He noticed the phone on the bedside table and was suddenly grave. 'You haven't used that?'

'No.'

'You realize how dangerous it would be to try to phone David? You haven't tried?'

'I've told you no.'

She was withdrawn again and he was finding it difficult to communicate with her. 'The flight is fixed up and I have all the necessary information. Tim took a trip to Normandy a few weeks ago and there's enough fuel in it to get us there tomorrow.'

'You told him we were going to Normandy?'

'No. Naturally not.'

'How will you get the plane back to him?'

'Well, I won't put the bloody thing in the post. He'll collect it, I suppose – eventually.'

'After we arrive in Normandy – what then?'

'I don't know. We'll have to play it by ear.'

'I haven't a passport. Isn't it illegal to land in another country like that?'

'Stop worrying. It will work out.'

'I don't see how it can.'

Neither did he, but he had been in difficult situations in the past

155

and had usually managed to struggle out of them. He went into the bathroom and tried the door. It was, as she had said, locked and there was no key in the keyhole. A bolt at the top of the door was stiff with dried on paint, but he managed to push it across. The bedroom door had an internal key. He locked it. He went back to the bathroom and took a shower. When he returned, she was lying on her side facing the window.

'Do you want me to sleep on the bed or in the bed?'

She was indifferent. 'It doesn't matter.'

Somewhile later he put the light out and got in beside her. She lay rigidly. He said gently, 'I won't touch you.'

She didn't answer.

He was the first to sleep, but he slept lightly and awoke shortly after two. One of the farm dogs had started to bark. He went over to the window and looked out. The moon was full and the hills looked white as if sprinkled with hoarfrost. Nothing moved.

He returned very quickly to the bed and she half awakened and moved over to him as she had in the old days. He held her to him, his hand in the small of her back. She said, 'David.' And then moving a little so that she could see him, 'David?'

'No. Sleep now.'

She recognized his voice, but didn't move away.

Just before dawn the dog barked again and they both awakened and listened to it. He wondered if the van had been discovered in the wood.

She said quietly, 'I'm frightened.'

'It's natural for the dog to bark.'

'Only if there are people around.'

'Or animals – there could be a fox.'

She leaned up on her elbow and looked down at him. 'It isn't too late for you to go back to them.'

'I'm not going back to them.'

'But why?'

156

'Because I choose to stay with you.'

'There isn't any love between us any more.'

He was silent. He was going with her into a wilderness of uncertainty. Love or lunacy – the word didn't matter very much.

She lay down again, her head on his outflung arm. 'You want me?'

'Yes.'

'Because I am any woman in bed with you?'

'Because you are in bed with me.'

She moved closer to him. 'And I want you – not loving you.'

'No,' he agreed, 'not loving me.' He kissed her gently on the throat and then on her breasts. She moved over and entwined her legs in his. The nightdress billowed across his face and she sat up and took it off.

She was half-smiling in the moonlight. 'Not loving you.'

'No.'

He took her as he had taken her in the height of their loving and it was as good as it had ever been. She lay back in his arms and traced the outline of his face with her finger. 'If we hadn't slept together we wouldn't have slept together.'

'Clearly not.'

'You're laughing at me.'

'Just smiling.'

'A natural act meaning nothing.'

'Nothing at all.'

She lay against him in a deep contentment that was like a small oasis of peace in a landscape of terror. Soon, she knew, her conscience would kick her until she was a mass of emotional bruises. Had David answered the phone when she made the call it wouldn't have happened. She had been answered by someone – one of the engineers – who said the bomb had brought the line down and that she couldn't be put through. She had been afraid to tell Mack when he asked her. It seemed pointless to tell him now. An abortive

157

phone call couldn't do either of them any harm.

'For a non-loving act of love,' he told her gently, 'it couldn't be bettered.'

It was after a leisurely breakfast and close on ten o'clock when Peggy walked with her over to the landing strip. Mack and Tim had already gone down to the plane and done the preliminary checking. It looked little more than a toy, Dee thought. A pretty aeroplane on a diminutive runway between fields of corn. The feeling of unreality was back with her again. It was possible to believe that she and Mack were going to take the plane up for a spin. It was possible to believe that they would return to the lunch that Peggy was about to cook for them. It was not possible to believe that she and Mack were going to climb into that silver and red contraption and fly out of England – perhaps for good.

If she could believe it she might feel something.

All she could feel was pleasure in the sunshine and in the smell of the grass. It was good to be alive. Mack had told her to bring her fur wrap and fold it over her toilet bag. To depart with a fur wrap, a face flannel, and a toothbrush, amused her. It was crazy. It wasn't happening. It wasn't true. She imagined David sitting in the un-bombed flat. She imagined going back to him in time for tea. She imagined the rush of guilt she had always felt in the past after sleeping with Mack and then seeing David again. It was all quite easy to imagine in a cool objective way. It wasn't at all easy to realize that she was on the run.

Peggy said, 'It's a nice day for your flight – not much wind and hardly any cloud. Now you've seen it, are you appalled at the prospect of flying in anything so small?'

'No. It's a pretty aeroplane.'

Peggy was amused. 'Don't tell Tim that – powerful – rugged – those are the words.'

'I'll remember.'

Mack, already in the cockpit, helped her up into the passenger seat. Tim, like the proud father of a mechanical genius, leaned in and pointed out the controls. 'That's the control column, it works the elevators and ailerons. That's the throttle lever. The pedals over there work the rudders.'

She didn't care how it worked. It smelt of aeroplane, warm and oily. She pretended for Tim's sake to take an interest in the instrument panel. 'It looks complicated.'

'You soon get used to it. Show her, Mack.'

Mack, anxious to get away but trying not to appear anxious, pointed out the airspeed indicator, the altimeter and the oil pressure and temperature gauges. He had made sure that the plane was fully tanked up. Now that he was in her again it felt like being in a familiar motor car. She was an easy little craft to pilot. Tim had told him how he had landed it a couple of times on one of the fields at the perimeter of the farm. Provided that the surface was reasonably flat she didn't need a runway. It was a piece of information he decided to use. They would be bound to run into officialdom eventually, but he would put off the evil moment as long as necessary.

Dee looked at him and smiled. He sensed that she battened down euphoria, ashamed to let it show. He tried to understand her mood. It was natural, he supposed, for days of deep depression and fear to be followed by a swing to the opposite extreme. But the fear should persist, for her own protection. The situation was real and nasty and the reality and nastiness of it would have to be faced up to. They weren't flying off to a never-never land, cosy, insulated and safe. There would be rain and cold and money running out and lies and deceit and the deceit was starting now.

Peggy said, 'Lunch in a couple of hours. I've a nice shoulder of lamb – one of our flock.'

Tim added, 'Poor little beast.'

Mack started the engine and waited for it to warm. He began to taxi down the runway.

159

England, he thought, familiar, small, green and pleasant land. It would have been nice to have spent a life-time in the Cotswolds. To farm here. To go home to undemanding, plain Peggy who was kind and liked to cook and who cherished her guests and warmed them with her hospitality. What good were the highlights? Too much pleasure. Too much pain. Tim hadn't been cursed with a questing, restless mind. He had never been touched with reforming zeal – or perhaps tainted was the better word. The people, as far as he was concerned, could muddle along as they had always muddled along. The cattle market was Tim's system, the herdsmen his Group. Good luck to him. He had chosen the better way.

He leaned over and waved. They were at the holding point at the end of the runway. The plane gathered up her power and began to rise.

Dee closed her eyes and pressed her hands against her stomach, and then the bird-free sensation took over and she opened her eyes and began to enjoy it. Tim and Peggy stood like peg dolls, motionless as if rooted to earth. She waved to them, wondering if she would ever see them again. Her sponge bag made a small mound under her wrap on her knee.

She said, 'I should feel like Judas, but I don't.'

He was busy at the controls, checking the instruments and raising the flaps. He answered calmly, 'It's a wrong analogy. We're not betraying them, just stealing their plane.'

'With handwaves and a promise to return for lunch – if that isn't betrayal, what is?'

'Deception. So your conscience isn't bothering you?'

'No. Is yours?'

'I have more important things to think about.'

She wished he would smile a little. The sky was blue and the plane was riding the wind and the sense of freedom was tingling through her like mead down a parched throat. She drank greedily of it. It was a delight. She had been resigned to death and now she was alive. All else was trivial.

'Mack?'

'Yes?'

'Our going away hasn't any finality. We'll come back. I feel it.'

'Yes, we'll come back.' He didn't feel it, he just hoped it would be possible. It was too late to regret everything that had happened. Remorse was a useless time-waster. He had taken her from a comfortable marriage, a comfortable home, and he had to do the best he could for her in reparation. The plane was flying easily as it always had done and he turned and looked at her.

She smiled at him. 'It's lovely.'

'Yes, she flies well.'

'I wish you'd stop worrying about me. I'm tough, young and optimistic. One day when I'm old I'll write my memoirs. I can just see the book on the bookstalls: How I Escaped the Group. Inside story of an attempt to overthrow the British Government.'

He didn't smile.

'They can't win, Mack. It couldn't happen. They're not as big and powerful as you think they are. When it's over I'll let David buy that cottage he wanted – or somewhere like it. If we can't have children, we'll adopt children.'

He didn't understand what a cottage had to do with children. He didn't understand her feelings for David. He wasn't fool enough to believe that the sexual pleasure they had had during the night would obliterate any deeply held affection she might have for David. If she followed her usual pattern she would start castigating herself for being unfaithful to him – or rather for being unfaithful to him and enjoying it so much. As for his own feeling for her, he knew now that it was more than caring and more than pleasure in bed. They had had days of misery together and her fear of him had hurt him more than he would have believed possible. At least that was over. She looked as if she would never be afraid of anything again. After

161

having touched the nadir she seemed to have been re-born. A rebirth into what, he wondered, and was afraid to think it through.

'Look down, Dee. We're about to cross the Channel.'

It was then that realization began to touch her. They were leaving England. The bouncy little plane was winging it like a seagull over the sea.

She said with less certainty, 'We'll come back.'

'Of course.'

She was silent watching the water far below. There was a lot of shipping in the Channel. It seemed hardly to move, but to lie on the sea like cardboard ships slotted into blue cardboard.

She wondered what she would have said to David if he had answered the phone last night. What kind of reassuring words do you say to a person when you are going away?

David, I'm going away, God knows where or for how long. I care about you.

Think about me.

I'll think about you. Always.

They were flying lower now and were getting close to the coast of France. There were long beaches. Children playing.

Mack put his hand over hers. 'Don't be sad.'

'I'm not.'

'Tim keeps his maps in that little cubbyhole on your side. Could you get them out? I want you to do some map reading for me.' She needed to have something to think about and do.

She said, 'There's a child down there – playing by himself – he seems so tiny – such a long way away – look, he's running to the water.'

'The maps, Dee.'

'He's seen us. Look, he's waving.'

She waved back, and then she tried to pull out the maps, but they were tightly wedged. She kept on pulling.

Down below the child saw the aeroplane glinting in the sun like

162

a shooting star and then it glowed bright red as a cracker sound splintered it into tiny pieces. It was beautiful and frightening and he stood in the sea and wept.

THIRTEEN

The Belvedere Nursing Home in Knightsbridge had once been an hotel. It had been bought and equipped by some of the wealthier Group members when the new system was just a feasible idea. Medical staff hadn't been difficult to recruit from the ailing Health Service. Not all were aware that they were being financed by a subversive political element, those that were became committed Group members.

Simon Warren, a consultant ophthalmologist, was even more committed than most, but even he baulked at what was being asked of him.

Once again he explained the situation to Admiral Jackson. 'The girl had corneal laceration due to fragments of glass. There's a prolapse of the iris. If the iris is prolapsed for any length of time there's a risk of its becoming necrotic and inflammation can cause blindness. The longer the operation is delayed the less chance there is of saving her sight.' He added, 'One eye is a write-off. It's essential I do all I can to save the other.'

'I'm asking you not to operate now. It's more than likely I shall ask you to operate in a few hours' time.'

'And what kind of vicious reprisal is that?' He had been present when Briony had come out of sedation sufficiently to confess that she had switched the briefcases. Unaware until then of the proposed bombing of the House of Commons he had been shocked.

'It's not a reprisal against the girl, though she deserves it. It's new pressure on Berringer. We can't muzzle French radio and they will be quick off the mark to report the plane crash. *The Galaxy* is preparing a front-page leader about tragic death of MP's wife just as soon as the story breaks.'

'You haven't told him about his wife's death?'

'Naturally not, but we can't keep him here indefinitely and the news can't be withheld indefinitely. Once he hears about the crash we'll have no hold over him.'

Warren's initiation into the Group's tactics had come some time ago. The escalation of violence as a kind of aversion therapy paving the way to the iron-handed discipline of totalitarianism he had been prepared to accept. Now that he was being presented with fact rather than theory he was shaken. It would be wise, he knew, not to show it.

'So the plane crash was an accident?'

The Admiral looked at him coolly. 'The plane crash was a mistake. Berringer carried what he thought was a bomb into the House. He complied. We didn't know that. Had he deliberately activated the bomb to kill Briony he would have been no further use to us. We want a front man we can mould. We can still mould him. He's emotionally motivated, that's his weakness. Briony quite obviously cares for him – more fool she. Even if he feels nothing for her it's not in his nature to stand by and allow her to lose her sight.'

'But you believe it's in my nature?'

The Admiral looked at the forty-year-old ophthalmologist and took his time to answer. When he did it was with a catalogue of facts. 'Your earning capacity here is treble what it was in the National Health Service. When we form the new Government there will be a modified health service directly under our control. You have a wife with expensive tastes and three children in boarding school. You can resign from the Belvedere if you wish. If you do, your chances of re-employment are slight. In this country they are nil.'

Warren's naturally fair skin was white and the long lines of strain running from his nostrils to his lips showed grey. 'To withhold my skill to the detriment of the patient is unethical.'

'Granted. But at this present time you can't afford ethics – anymore than the Group can afford ethics. You don't build a new political system on a pious foundation of Old Testament commandments. We're not constructing a monastery. We use what bricks we have to hand. If the bricks are somewhat dirty then that's too bad. All we're concerned with is their strength.'

'You're using a lot of dirty bricks to shove under the feet of one reluctant man. For God's sake, why Berringer? Surely there are others?'

'Berringer inspires confidence in the people. He has a unique gift of empathy. There's a strong rapport between himself and the public. He has the kind of personality that cuts across party politics. Both sides of the House get along with him. Under the present democratic system – if it were to survive – he would eventually become Prime Minister. Under our new system he will achieve that rank immediately.'

'In a puppet capacity.'

'To what extent is any Prime Minister free? The extent to which Berringer is controlled will depend on him. Eventually he will be as committed as any of us.'

'Even though the Group murdered his wife?'

The Admiral shrugged. 'Mrs Berringer's death was due to the incompetence of Mackilroy. He hadn't flown a plane for sometime. There was a mechanical defect and he didn't know how to cope.'

Warren smiled thinly. 'The evidence to the contrary being in the sea.'

'Quite. It shouldn't be difficult to persuade Mackilroy's farming friend to come forward to explain how Mackilroy and Mrs Berringer spent a night together at the farm and to say in what perfect health and spirits Mrs Berringer was. Berringer was never sure – in the early days – whether or not he was being hoaxed and cuckolded. He shouldn't find that alternative explanation difficult to accept. There was never, in fact, any violence.'

'Apart from the end.'

The Admiral didn't answer. On the whole, he thought, the way things had gone so far was not the fiasco it had first seemed. Briony had let the bomb off in the flat by activating it when she thought she was de-activating it, but her stupidity had brought excellent publicity to Berringer. *The Galaxy* had already gone to town on that. If Berringer had needed an alibi of innocence then this was it. When the original plan was put into operation again later today – this time without Berringer playing an active part – he would be justifiably away from the House after suffering from what seemed a similar attempt on his life. Public sympathy fanned by the *Galaxy*'s rhetoric would never be stronger than it was now. The time for action couldn't be more ripe.

'What I want you to do,' he said to the surgeon 'is to explain the necessity of an operation and stress the urgency of it. You don't have to deliver an ultimatum. Leave that part of it to me. Get one of your staff to fetch him in now.'

Warren hesitated on the verge of protest then, thinking better of it, went over to the intercom. Berringer had been on mild sedatives since he had come into the Belvedere with the girl, their effect however would have worn off by now.

He said, 'I shall explain the necessary surgery, as you force me to. After that I shall leave the two of you together. If I'm told to withhold surgery then the decision is yours and Berringer's – not mine.'

Thus spake Pilate, he thought.

David had been sitting at Briony's bedside for hours in a kind of timeless limbo. He was dry-mouthed, stiff and tired but only vaguely aware of his own discomfort. His thoughts were wholly centred on her. When he saw her immediately after the bomb blast he thought she couldn't possibly survive. That she had – and would – seemed to him a major miracle. The blast had deafened her, but it was only a temporary deafness. Most of her face was swathed in bandages, but the cuts were superficial – apart from the cuts to her eyes. If this were a kind of divine justice, he thought, then any remaining belief he might have in a God of compassion was killed stone dead.

She was too weak to do anything more than whisper, but it was like a voice crying out in the wilderness. She was very frightened. He kept her hand in his, gently pressing it when he sensed she needed reassuring that he was there. When the nurse came and told him that the ophthalmologist wanted to see him in his consulting room he was reluctant to leave her. He tried to disengage his hand, but her fingers tightened on his.

He brought his face down close to hers. 'I'll be back as quickly as I can be. The eye surgeon wants to see me.' He was afraid to hold out hope and afraid to withhold it. 'Everything possible will be done.'

Her words came out weakly and with effort. 'I . . . can't . . . hear . . . you.'

'I'll be back soon.'

She heard that 'Stay . . . please . . . dark like night . . . can't breathe.'

The nurse was still in the room. 'I'll give her something to calm her.' She was brisk, efficient and too well trained to show her disquiet over the delayed operation.

David sat down again by the bed. 'Tell the consultant to come and see me here. I'm staying.'

He put his lips close to Briony's ear. 'You're all right. Quite safe. I won't go.'

He knew her well enough to get inside her mind. Her obsessional fear of blindness lay acutely along his senses. He remembered how she had sat in the darkness in the flat when she had heard that one of the Silver Swan victims had been blinded. Her conscience festered inside her like a disease, he doubted whether she would ever be whole. In order to save him from the same agony she had weighted his own briefcase with a couple of onyx ashtrays and changed its position on the study table so that he had picked it up believing it to be the bomb. All this had come out in fragmented conversation over a long time. Fearing that she had accidentally activated the bomb she had been on her way to warn the occupants of the basement flat when it had exploded. If she had stayed where she was she would have been killed. At this moment she would have preferred that alternative. She would rather be dead than blind. He knew that quite clearly.

The possible reprisal of the bombing on Dee had worried him acutely. It was unlikely that that aspect had occurred to Briony. When she had eventually been able to speak her first words were to absolve him. She was afraid of what they might do to him. What they might do to Dee or to her, probably didn't impinge on her mind.

The Admiral and the surgeon came in quietly and he swung round in his chair to face them. He wished to God that Jackson would take himself off. That he was being held in the Belvedere like a prisoner in Brixton jail was perfectly clear to him. It was all very civilized, of course. It was better, he was told, that he should use the facilities of the nursing home than to go an hotel. It suited him to be near Briony so he hadn't jibbed. He wondered what their next move would be.

He was soon to find out.

Admiral Jackson was the first to speak. 'I didn't want to hold this conversation in front of the girl, but Mr Warren assures me she can't hear as long as we speak quietly. It might be better, Berringer, if you left the bedside and drew your chair a little away.'

David refused. 'She needs the contact of my hand.'

The Admiral had gone over to the window and was standing with his back to it. The mid-afternoon sun blazed strongly from a dark blue sky and he looked like a figure in stained glass, outlined in brightness but with features in shadow. The surgeon took one of the easy chairs and angled it so that he wasn't directly looking at the girl in the bed.

He spoke very quietly. 'It's normal practice for a consent form to be signed by a relative before an operation if the patient herself can't sign. Briony has no family. Admiral Jackson has stood in as loco parentis for the girl since the death of her parents. If he signs the consent form I will operate.'

David said, 'Yes – well . . .?'

'One of Briony's eyes is beyond saving. The other has a major laceration of the cornea with a prolapsed iris. The surgical procedure is to excise the prolapsed tissue. If this isn't done quickly the prolapsed tissue becomes necrotic and inflammation can cause blindness. The operation shouldn't be delayed.'

David sensed the underlying tension which was rather more than normal concern. 'I don't understand. Is there a problem? Why should the operation be delayed? Isn't she strong enough physically for it?

'Yes, she's strong enough. And there's a fair chance of saving her sight.'

'Then why the hesitation?'

The surgeon looked away from him and at Jackson. 'I have a theatre in readiness and it will be held that way. You'll find me in my consulting room as soon as you know.' He turned back to David. 'You understand what I'm saying? If I had full professional freedom I would have performed the operation with or without consent before now. If it is delayed too long then . . .' He looked towards the bed and didn't say it.

David understood.

He was silent as rage built up in him. Briony's hand moved under his and he realized that his grip had hurt her. He relaxed the pressure and her fingers curled in his palm, her nails sharp on his skin.

The surgeon stood up and pushed back his chair. He went over to the door without another word and it closed quietly behind him.

The Admiral, anticipating an outburst, tried to stall it. 'I don't know to what extent the bomb blast has deafened her, but that will right itself on its own. Her sight is different. Do you want to hold the rest of the conversation out in the corridor?'

'No. Say what you have to say here. She can't hear unless I bring my face down to hers . . . What has happened to Dee?'

The Admiral was startled but tried not to show it. 'Why should you assume that anything has happened to your wife?'

Relief diminished the rage a little. 'Because you are bringing more pressure to bear. What more do you want of me? A second performance of what happened yesterday?' If you do, he thought, then God help Dee, Briony, all of us. He couldn't voluntarily take that gallows walk twice.

'No, I don't ask that of you. Every man has his limits and you reached yours yesterday. You're not a man of violence. The Group wants to build you up, not break you.'

'Then on what terms do you consent to the operation?'

'That you make a broadcast at six o'clock this evening pledging your support to the new system and urging the British public to do likewise.'

'The new system? Meaning . . .?'

'Yes. About ten minutes ago. It should have been May Day, but it will go down in history as May Day plus one. This time the responsibility was Pruet's.' He turned and looked out of the window. 'It's strange how life goes on quite normally even when the course of history has been changed. We didn't hear the bomb.

Neither did those people down in the street. They're going about their business quiet calmly and collectedly. When you speak to them this evening you will stress that they continue to behave calmly and sensibly. At this present moment our military task force is taking up key positions. The country is under martial surveillance. As yet, unobtrusive. The future conduct of the people will depend largely on you. You can ease them from the laxity of democratic government into the dynamic progressiveness of the new system. We don't want a revolution on our hands. A slow peaceful change-over is possible under your leadership.' He smiled. 'Don't look as if a chasm has opened under your feet. It's still the same country and you've been offered to play a major rôle in it. The sick man of Europe is about to have the strongest injection of anti-subversive terrorism it has ever known. It will become strong and powerful again – above all it will become disciplined . . . And don't look at me as if I am a devil with horns. The system will work positively towards good. The aims of the Group when you are fully conversant with them will equate with your conscience.'

David, sick to the gut and appalled, hardly recognized his own voice. 'How many were killed in the House?'

'I don't know. I can't give you details of that yet. The leaders of the main parties won't survive – if they have already survived. Neither will any of the stronger members who might carry some weight with the people. The British public believe that they have been deprived of government – not by the Group – but by whatever terrorist organization they are most afraid of. All enemies of the State will be exposed by us – and purged by us. There will be some initial bloodshed.'

'As in Nazi Germany.'

'We are not at war with Jews.'

'As in Russia.'

'There is no parallel.'

173

'Apart from your methods. You torture my wife. You would let this girl go blind.'

'I never tortured your wife. Her screams were due to a rat on her bed. When she wrote your name she wrote it with her left hand.'

'I don't believe you.'

'I didn't expect you to, but it happens to be true. You'll have proof of the truth of it later – when you see her.' He said it quite blandly, the lie didn't bother him in the slightest.

Hope flared. 'When do I see her and where?'

'You'll have details of that after the broadcast. And Briony will be operated on after the broadcast.'

'If I agree to the broadcast will you permit Briony to be operated on now?'

The Admiral smiled derisively. 'Don't take me for a fool. Briony will go to the operating theatre after you have made your speech to the British public this evening. Keep sitting beside her and thinking about it. I'll come for your answer at five.'

For the first hour after the Admiral had gone Briony slept. Her hand was relaxed and he put it gently under the covers and then fearing that she might wake and go through the suffocating panic of awakening into darkness he put his own hand under the covers and held it again. He kept on seeing the shambles of the House in his mind. He remembered his conversation with Miller yesterday. At least Miller's son and girl friend wouldn't be there. But there would have been other innocent spectators there. People like Dee. He thought, Oh God, Dee, my lovely one, what am I to do? What else could I have done? How could I have acted positively to avert the horror of the explosion in the House and at the same time ensure your safety? He tried to re-cap all his actions over the last few day and wondered how he might have acted differently. If he had cared less for Dee . . . If he had been more inclined to take risks . . . if – bloody – if . . . He couldn't fight a Juggernaut. He couldn't even put up a token resistance to it. While Dee was held he could do damn all. He had to ride along with it – pay it lip service – watch its wheels crush, maim and kill. Its vision of a super-race was Hitlerian. That had sounded plausible in the early days, too. The concentration camps had come later. No system that began with mass-murder could evolve into anything worth while. It seemed to him extraordinary that people like Mackilroy could be conned into believing in it – and people like the surgeon who had kept his eyes carefully averted from Briony. His conscience quite obviously had worried him.

He reached up behind the bed and rang the bell. After a few minutes a nurse came in. He hadn't seen this one before. She was young, about the same age as Briony. He asked her if she would sit and hold Briony's hand. 'I have to go and see Mr Warren. She needs to know that there is someone in the room with her. Will you stay?'

The nurse who hadn't been briefed to the contrary said of course she would stay. She also directed him to Warren's consulting room.

Warren, too, had been sitting in deep thought and he looked up angrily when David came in. 'I don't see what good any further conversation can do.'

David glanced around the opulently furnished room with its soft carpeting and pale panelled walls. There was an abstract painting in tones of brown and grey behind the desk. He said, 'Briony wouldn't like that.'

'What are you talking about?'

'Briony's interest in art.' He pulled out a chair for himself and sat down. 'When she was fifteen she painted a parakeet and sold the painting for five pounds. She told me that when we were sitting in the Dulwich park, not so very long ago.'

'And why are you telling me now?'

'Isn't it obvious?'

'Yes, it's obvious, but it won't do any good.' There was a bottle of Scotch in his desk drawer. He had been resisting it all the afternoon and intended to go on resisting it. It wasn't easy.

175

David said, 'She likes her colours bright. Her ambition is to study art. Even if she finished up in gaol for her part in the Silver Swan bombing, art classes wouldn't be denied her. We're not a ruthless nation. We understand compassion. We don't withhold sight when we have the power to give it.'

'We – meaning who? Particularize. Don't come at me with woolly arguments. You're living in today. Not in yesterday.' It was bitter.

'Meaning the majority of the British public who haven't been brainwashed into believing that a bunch of maniacs can offer them a better way of life.'

'Maniacs? It depends how you define sanity. The Group is extremely well organized and extremely powerful.'

'And extremely rich. It owns the Belvedere, I suppose?'

'Yes.'

'And other private hospitals like it?'

'Yes.'

'And it owns you.'

Warren said smoothly, 'If you're trying to rattle me, you're not succeeding. The Belvedere pays my salary.'

'Which is a thumping sight larger than the salary you had when you had clinical freedom under the State.'

'I have clinical freedom here apart from this one issue.'

'And this one issue, as you call it, is a negligible one?'

'I didn't say that.'

'You're shocked and extremely worried.'

'I didn't say that either.'

'You don't have to. It shows.'

David noticed a framed photograph on the desk. He pulled it towards him and turned it around. It showed an attractive smiling woman with dark hair worn in a fringe. It also showed a boy of about fifteen, a younger boy, and a girl of about nine with fair hair like the man sitting opposite.

'Your family?'

'Yes, my family – and don't try an emotional argument, it won't work.'

'I've no intention of becoming emotional – still less pleading with you. I'd offer you money if I'd sufficient to compensate you for what you'd lose if you left here. That's the threat, I suppose?'

Warren didn't answer.

'And so you won't operate – or you will when it's too late. You'll stay on here and you'll have clinical freedom – up to a point. Briony now. Someone else later. You will continue to live well, but perhaps you won't sleep so well. You'll be an excellent husband and father from the material point of view. Your family won't want for anything that money can buy. But there's a lot it can't buy. Peace of mind, for instance . . . You've heard about the bomb in the House of Commons, I suppose?'

'Yes.'

'But you won't burden the conscience of your family with it?'

'Why should I? They're not responsible.'

'But you accept that responsibility for yourself?'

'As a Group member – yes.'

'You knew it was going to happen?'

'No.'

David believed him. 'But you condone it?'

The surgeon was silent.

'Out there,' David said, 'the majority of the public wouldn't condone it either – if they knew. The Group is still a minority. They're still feeling for power. You're helping them towards it by allowing a girl to become blind. It's a strange route to the top, isn't it?'

He stood up. The man was immovable, but he had tried. 'I suppose you'd regard Briony as a casualty along the way – and my wife another casualty. Briony loses her sight. My wife has a maimed hand. I care for both of them and because I care for both of them

I shall make that broadcast this evening. What the hell else can I do?'

He went over to the door and paused a moment. He thought that Warren had been about to say something. But he was mistaken. The surgeon looked back at him silently.

When he returned to Briony she was awake and the nurse was trying to calm her. 'He's here now.'

David leaned over the bed. 'I'm with you.' She moved her head restlessly on the pillows.

The nurse said, 'She's been trying to remove the bandages. Can you cope?'

'Yes. Until I have to go. I'll ring for you when I need you again.'

He brought his mouth down to Briony's ear. 'You're going to be operated on in a few hour's time. What you have to do now is try to stay calm.'

'It's . . . like . . . a . . . pit.' Her hands were opening and closing convulsively. He held them in his.

'When . . . I dream . . . I see . . .' He rubbed the ball of his thumb on her knuckles.

'And . . . then . . . I wake . . . a nightmare . . .'

'Not for long.' He repeated it, making sure she heard. 'Not for long.'

'Don't . . . leave me . . . again.'

'I have to. I can't go into the operating theatre with you.'

'I wish . . . you would . . . stay . . . always.'

Oh God, he thought, oh my dear God. There had never been any softness or affection between them. Had they slept together during those brief moments of strong physical attraction, they would have done so without tenderness. He had given her no quarter and she had slammed back hard. It was different now. Her face was a crisscross of surgical tape under the thick band of gauze over her eyes. Even her mouth had been cut by flying glass. He bent down and very gently kissed it.

FOURTEEN

The television studio was hot and stuffy as if the air conditioning wasn't working. He remembered the previous time he had been there. It seemed like a century ago. He had given a good performance then. He would have to give an even better one now, but doubted if he could drum up any thoughts about anything. Leo Carradine was seated on his left and the news announcer on his right. Beyond the announcer was a man he had only just been introduced to – Brigadier Gregory Harringford. He sat there in full military regalia, a tall thin white-haired man with an air of quiet command made humane by a slow smile that crinkled up his eyes.

Strength, David thought. Humanitarianism. An avuncular militarism. A good image. The public might be fool enough to fall for it.

He wished the lights here weren't so bright. The make-up girl had insisted on putting a lotion on his face – an astringent to stop the sweat. His skin felt stretched. He put his hand up to feel it and saw that his hand was wet with sweat, too. Normally he was dry skinned. The BBC news-producer had offered him a drink before he came into the studio, but the Admiral had declined on his behalf before he could answer. There was too much at stake to make a balls-up of it.

He had left the Belvedere with the Admiral at five o'clock. The operation was scheduled for eight, provided the broadcast went

179

well. He had been given no definite time of his meeting with Dee. The Admiral had replied irritably to his persistent questioning that he would see her sometime soon.

They were not on the air yet and Carradine aware of his nerves tried to make conversation. '*The Galaxy* gave an excellent account of the bombing of your flat. Did you see it?'

'Yes.' The Admiral had shown it to him after the briefing when they were sitting waiting to come into the studio. The account covered the front page. He remembered the headline. 'Terror'. Just the one word in large black letters. Under it was a picture of the flat and a picture of him – the same one that they had used after his last broadcast. Under the headline was 'Berringer escapes death', followed by several paragraphs denouncing the growing anarchy of the country and calling for firm government. Parts of his last speech were quoted. 'This quiet, firm, far-seeing politician with all the qualities of leadership is one of the few remaining hopes of the country', the blurb had gone on, 'heed him. His escape from death was providential. We have much to be thankful for'. *The Galaxy* had no evening edition. He wondered what they would use for a headline tomorrow when they wrote about the bombing in the House. Chaos? No, that would suit the evening papers due to come out now. Tomorrow's headline would have to be more constructive. He tried writing it in his mind using the pious bishop style of pulpit language that *The Galaxy* favoured, and mentally sketched a cartoon figure of himself, nimbus awry, two fingers raised in a blessing turned the wrong way round. In moments of stress his thoughts seemed to splinter off and come together in the form of idiotic images. He realized he was smiling.

Carradine asked him if he were all right.

'Perfectly.'

'Nerves take people different ways. There's water in the carafe if you want it.'

'I don't.'

180

Carradine pushed a quarto-sized piece of typing paper towards him. 'If your mind dries up, then read from these notes. You'll see the same notes on that teleprompter screen over there.' He pointed it out. 'Don't look at the notes unless you have to. You're a remarkably good speaker when you let yourself get into the mood of it. Some of your rhetoric in the House has been first class.'

The newscaster said that they had a couple of minutes. He, too, asked David if he were all right. 'The news is quite bloody, I know. I only wish I didn't have to announce it. You come in with what you have to say immediately after me. The Brigadier comes in last. OK?'

'Yes.'

'Right.'

The cameras began closing in.

They were on the air. Several million people, David thought, with their eyes glued to the box were waiting to be conned. Waiting to be conned by him. He was only half listening to the announcer's voice: 'At three-fifteen this afternoon a bomb exploded in the Chamber of the House of Commons. It is feared that the death toll is tragically high. The House at the time of the explosion was packed with spectators in the public gallery. Rescue attempts are still in progress as with the collapse of the main walls of the Chamber those not killed by the explosion are trapped by debris.' The announcement was followed by a period of silence as the cameras showed the precincts of the House and the gathering crowds outside the police cordon. A reporter on the spot took up the story:

'I have been standing here for the last couple of hours and any optimism I might have had at the start has gradually been eroded as the news has come through. The damage is not obvious externally so don't be fooled by what you see on your screens. The Chamber had been completely demolished. No one as yet has been brought out alive and the chances of anyone being brought out alive are

181

exceedingly remote. All the public services are here, and all are working flat out in the most appalling conditions to try to get through to what is described as a pure hell of destruction. Whoever planted the bomb timed it with diabolical precision. It will be a miracle if any of the leaders of the nation have survived and as I stand here I'm fast losing faith in miracles. The mood of the people is ugly and who can blame them? They're quiet and controlled as they watch and wait, but I can feel their anger like a gathering storm.' He paused and then added on a quieter note that he would relay news of casualties as they came through and was handing back to the studio for the time being.

The newscaster took it on from there. 'The police have asked us to advise you to stay away from the Westminster area for the next few hours. Information may be obtained if you phone the number appearing on your screen now. The number will be shown again at the end of the bulletin. News of casualties will be given as it comes through to us. In the meantime, I have seated beside me here in the studio Mr David Berringer who only yesterday escaped a similar attempt on his life at his Kensington flat. He has come here directly from the Belvedere Nursing Home in order to speak to you during this period of grave national crisis. Mr Berringer . . .'

David felt the sweat on his hands go cold. His tongue was dry. The images in his brain levelled out into a flat plane of nothingness. Carradine very quietly said, 'The teleprompter, read it . . .'

He looked up at the screen. The words were solid and black like a notice of an execution. He began slowly to read them.

'When I spoke to you last I spoke of the growing canker in the country. I warned you of the consequences to this once great island of ours if the canker were not cut out at source. Today the tentacle of evil has reached the very heart of our government. The perpetrators of this monstrous outrage must be named and made to suffer for the evil they had done. Britain in the war years was at her weakest and yet at her strongest because the enemy was not within her ranks.

The enemy is within your ranks now – in your office – on your factory floor – in the house next door – in the street. You must close your ranks against him. Under normal circumstances I would have been in the House of Commons today and I would have died with my fellow politicians. I have been spared to serve you. I have been spared to lead you out of the chaos into a better more disciplined way of life. I have been spared to . . .'

The newscaster's phone rang and cut him off in mid-sentence. He leaned back in his chair, surprised that his tongue had fumbled out the words this far, thankful for a temporary respite.

The newscaster apologized briefly, 'It's probably more news of casualties from Westminster . . .' He listened and made an irritable gesture. 'Surely not now . . .' He looked at David, hesitated and was about to put the phone down when David took it from him.

'A call for me?'

'Yes.'

David said into the mouthpiece, 'Well?'

It was Simon Warren. He gave his news quickly. 'It's just to tell you that I operated on Briony as soon as you and the Admiral left the premises. The extra few hours should help. She will have impaired vision, but at least she will see. I thought you should know. There's something else you should know, and I can't cushion it for you. There isn't time. Your wife and Mackilroy were killed in an attempt to fly to France this morning. He was probably trying to save her from a reprisal after the bombing. There was a bomb in the plane. Her death wasn't an accident. Now say what you think you have to say – or don't say anything. And good luck.' The line went dead.

Shock held him suspended in time so that even his heart beat seemed stilled and then it began to beat again like a sledge hammer in his chest. The cameras, like the microscopes of scientists, watched dispassionately as the agony surged through each fibre of his body so that he felt one vast pain. A pain that killed personality. Brain. The sum-total of himself.

Dee.

Someone was putting something cold into his hand. Water from the carafe. He felt his fingers like ice on the glass.

Dee.

A plane crash.

Murder.

The word prodded his mind into life. Murder. They had murdered Dee.

He tried to disbelieve it. She had been dead all these hours and he hadn't known it. It wasn't possible. He would have known it. At the moment of her dying he would have known it.

But he hadn't.

And it was true.

Warren had told him the truth. Just as he had told him the truth about Briony. Warren had done the unpredictable and smashed his own career to hell so that he could speak to those people out there now and smash the Group to hell. Or die . . . trying.

Carradine said, 'We're temporarily off the air. 'What's the matter? What were you told?'

He was suddenly immensely calm. 'Nothing I can't handle. Let's get on with it. This time without the monitor.'

Carradine leaned over and conferred with the Brigadier. He shrugged and nodded.

The newscaster spoke to the nearest camera. 'As you can see by Mr Berringer the news we keep receiving from the site of the bombing is extremely shocking. Are you ready to continue, Mr Berringer?'

His voice was as cold as the tumbler in his hand. 'Quite ready.' He took a sip of water before putting the tumbler down.

'Until I received the phone call just now I was reading to you from a teleprompter screen. Many of the sentiments I expressed were perfectly valid sentiments. The country has been bedevilled for a long time by various factions. We have been harassed by bombs and weakened by strikes. But nothing has happened yet that we can't contain. Democracy may seem little better than a dog-fight to you at times. Parliamentary bickering may seem like the nonsense of children. Some of you today when you heard of the bomb in the House might have even felt relief that the dog-fights and the bickering were at an end. Good, you might have said. Now for something better. The country needs discipline, you might have said. And for discipline where do you look? Towards the end of my talk to you I am to introduce you to Brigadier Gregory Harringford who is seated on the right of the Newscaster. He is – shall we say – the strong arm of the new government. Oh yes, you are going to have a strong new government, but before you say Sieg Heil to it let me make it clear to you what you are getting. You are getting a military backed neo-Fascist set-up that is neither better nor worse than a comparable Communist set-up which is equal and opposite. You might eventually thrive under either extreme. You might even find some good in either extreme. You'll also find bad. Your new masters – if you accept them – operate under the innocuous title of the Group. Don't let the title mislead you. They are strong and they are powerful. Their aim, they say, is to bring a new discipline to the country. Their method is to escalate violence so that you will readily accept their new discipline. Many of the recent bombings attributed to other sources have been theirs. The bomb in the House of Commons today was theirs. Under pain of death to my wife who was held hostage to them I have been forced to speak to you on their behalf. I apologize to you for having deceived you in my earlier broadcast and in the first part of my talk to you this evening. The phone call just now was to say that my wife had died in an air-crash. It was an act of reprisal because I had seemingly disobeyed orders and refused to cause the devastation in the House of Commons that was caused one day later – today. I did, in fact, carry what I thought was a bomb in to the House yesterday. By the grace of God and the courage of a young girl who was nearly blinded by the explosion in my flat, I haven't that on my conscience. But it nearly happened – and it wasn't my courage or, I regret to say, my patriotism that prevented it. Priorities may be evaluated intellectually but when there is a personal factor one behaves in the only way that seems possible – appalling as that way may be. My wife now is dead and they have no further hold over me. I am free to tell you to get off your backsides and fight for what you know. And what you know is freedom. Democracy isn't a dirty word and it isn't a shining image of perfection either. It's a fair and feasible way of life and to my way of thinking better than any alternative. I don't know how long I shall be allowed to live after speaking to you as I have spoken now and quite frankly I don't at this moment care, but as long as I draw breath I shall walk free – my own path – my own ideas – my own words.' He stopped and turned towards the Brigadier. 'And now – in our as yet free country where free speech is still allowed – I give you the opposing view, Brigadier?'

The Brigadier, white-faced, sat for a few moments in silence and then he got up and went out.

Carradine said sharply, 'Get the bloody programme off the air.'

David didn't expect to leave Broadcasting House unmolested, but no-one touched him. It would happen, he knew, sooner or later. He didn't know what good his words would do. Some good, hopefully. The country now would be on its mettle. It would know its enemy, if not by name and face, then by deed.

By deed.

A bomb in an aircraft.

He stood on the pavement outside Broadcasting House. The air was wet with recent rain and the evening sky was building up pale grey cumulous clouds against a backdrop of oyster.

He couldn't weep for Dee. His grief was a dry hard pain. He tried not to think of Mackilroy. The days of their incarceration together would always be a mystery to him. Perhaps it was better that way. In the end he had tried to save her. He owed him that much gratitude. Gratitude? Stupid word. Mackilroy had been an usurper. He had sat in the plane and died with her. That should have been his privilege.

To die.

What did it mean to die?

He couldn't believe that she had gone from him finally. To understand that would take a long time. It was unlikely, he thought, that he would ever understand. As from now his time would be short.

He had arrived at Broadcasting House in the Admiral's car. He hailed a passing cab and told the driver to take him to the Kensington flat. Once there he didn't know why he had come. This gaping blackened structure under police guard was no part of any pilgrimage to the past to find Dee. She had been there once and was there no longer. Briony's impression was on it now. A devastation of rubble created by love. It was a traiterous thought and one he refused to harbour.

He went back to the cab. 'Westminster. The Houses of Parliament.'

The cabby had recognized him. 'To see where the bomb dropped, Mr Berringer? I can't bring you up close.'

'As close as you can.'

The area was full of ambulances and police cars. He paid off the cabby and began walking. Policemen marked off an area through which the general public was not allowed to pass. He would have been allowed through, but he didn't press the privilege. Those days were gone – as his home had gone. He thought of his friends on both sides of the House. The place had an unique atmosphere of friendship and enmity and withal was extraordinarily comfortable to the spirit like a familiar glove on one's hand.

Dee's glove.

187

Perfumed and soft.

It had given him strength to destroy. Destruction through love. Thank God this destruction now was not of his doing. The air was bitter with the dust that billowed through the broken windows and cracked fabric of the external walls.

He was about to go when he heard his name. 'Berringer.' And then someone else took it up. 'Berringer. Berringer.' The people around him began to turn towards him and then to press in on him. His name was becoming a chant so that the syllables were broken up. Berr – in – ger . . . Berr – in – ger.' It was getting louder like the steady thump of a drum-beat.

He hadn't expected the Group to send a lynch mob. Self-preservation made him back slowly away so that he was pressed up against the people behind him. They were yelling his name now, 'Berringer.'

And then rough hands held him and he was hoisted up on to someone's shoulder. The mob was pushing through the police cordon and the police couldn't stop it. They were taking him into the precinct of the House, past the ambulances and the stretcher bearers and then up to the door. There, like a surging tide against a narrow entrance to a cave, they stopped.

It was just, he thought, even desirable. If it had to happen then let it happen here. He tried not to show fear. He had not believed that he cared sufficiently for life now to feel it. But he did.

The impetus over, the crowd was silent. One looked to the other waiting for the word. And then it came quietly from somewhere at the back of the crowd. 'Lead us.'

'Help us.'

'Tell us what to do.'

And then silence again. Total silence as they waited.

He felt tears at the back of his throat and for a long time couldn't speak. And then the words burst from him harsh and strong: 'Resist. Show your strength. Don't capitulate. Fight!'

188

And they took up the word Fight and yelled their approval so that the whine of the bullet was lost in the uproar. The sudden blackness struck him like nightfall.

189

FIFTEEN

The room held a trestle bed, some cheap kitchen furniture and a fridge. Foster crushed ice cubes into a towel and placed it at the nape of David's neck. He apologized in his high, thin voice. 'You were hit rather too hard, but it was necessary to remove you and you wouldn't have come willingly. The man holding you was shot through the head. Bad marksmanship. The bullet was intended for you.'

He smiled sourly. What had Berringer intended, he wondered? To march the mob through the streets of London? Back to Broadcasting House, perhaps, to tear Harringford and Jackson and his minions limb from limb? One of his own minions had used the butt of his pistol on him as he had fallen into the crowd. And then the machine guns had opened up. It was against the odds that they had got him out. Miracles sometimes happened.

David was in the grip of nausea following concussion. The words weren't registering. That Foster of the Secret Intelligence Service had somehow removed him to this place and was apologizing for the method was the only fact he could grasp. He remembered vaguely his original intention of calling on Foster on the night he had learnt of the bomb – and then thinking better of it. For Dee's sake he had walked away.

For Dee's sake.

Realization with returning consciousness hit him anew so that he bent double with the physical pain of her loss.

Foster, not understanding, apologized again. 'We had to get you out of the melee. It was the only way. People were falling around you like sheep in an abattoir. You had the kind of anger in you that invited martyrdom. And what damn use is a martyr?' He poured a measure of whisky into a tumbler. 'I don't know if this is good for a slug on the head – or bad for it.' He handed over the tumbler and David took it and sipped the contents slowly. It burnt through his sickness, easing it slightly.

He said quietly, 'Dee is dead.'

Foster looked away. 'I know. I'm sorry.'

'I tried to come to you.'

'I know that, too.'

'Then why didn't you come to me?'

'Because you haven't the monopoly of distrust. We didn't know the degree of your commitment. We couldn't take chances.'

'How much did you know?'

'Then? Not enough.'

David got off the bed and walked groggily over to the window. The night was dark and he could see his own reflection in the glass, and in the room behind him Foster, aquiline featured, thin short grey hair, dressed in city pin-stripes, immaculately groomed, looking back at him.

'So the night when the Atkinson woman told me about the bomb – had I not dithered on your doorstep . . .?'

Foster shrugged. 'Old ground now. Leave it. Accept the situation as it is.' He wondered if he should reveal how close the SIS had been to springing Dee on the day she left the cottage. When he had parked at the cross-roads he had been optimistic of the outcome. But . . . A matter of minutes. A herd of cows. Incidents that had changed the pattern irrevocably. It was better that he shouldn't know. Mackilroy dead and Dee alive – that was the intention. They had had their tabs on Stringer for sometime. If Stringer had talked faster and sooner and they had located the cottage with minutes to spare then Berringer would be a loving grateful husband again not this fighting-wounded, fool-hardy leader-figure who had had to be hijacked here for his own safety.

He suggested he should come away from the window. 'Or pull down the blind.'

David moved away impatiently. 'Where is this place?'

'Battersea. A small terraced house.'

'You have a lot of explaining to do.'

'I know.' Foster fetched a tumbler and poured some whisky for himself. 'The Home Office,' he said, 'behaves sometimes with the sluggishness of an obese old crone but when the sniff of danger begins to penetrate the brain cells it comes slowly to life. We haven't been exactly sitting on our arses during the last few months. The situation isn't as bad as it seems.'

'There's been a massacre in the House of Commons. How could it be worse?'

'My latest information is that the destruction isn't total. That outside broadcaster made it sound worse than it is. It seems you'll have the remnants of a Cabinet. They didn't all die.'

'Not yet.'

'They will be guarded – as you are guarded. There are safe houses in the City. This is one of them. Reasonably impenetrable. There's one of our men on the stairs and a couple more on the ground-floor. Later, when we gain control, we'll move you somewhere more comfortable.'

'You'll move me?' It was proprietorial. Suspicion flared. He had suspected Foster earlier. The situation was still the same, why should he take Foster at face value now?

Foster read his expression correctly. 'The most virulent disease that's going to be around for a long time is the disease of doubt. I'm not a Group member.'

'I only have your word for that. You could be holding me here

193

at Jackson's command. You could be the executioner.'

'I could be. I have a loaded point thirty-eight in my pocket.'

'Intended for me?'

'Not intended to be used on you.'

'Prove it.'

'I can't. You'll learn to trust me in your own time.' Foster sat silent for several minutes studying the man opposite him. Berringer had thrown the wet towel aside and the ice had melted into the collar of his shirt. 'Does your head still hurt you?'

'Damn my head.'

Foster smiled. 'It would have been unfortunate if your skull had been fractionally thinner.' He became serious again. 'The only pistol that will be used on you with lethal intent will be held by a Group member, and that can only happen if you leave the safety of this room before the time is right.'

'And when will the time be right?'

Foster chose his words carefully. 'When the Group hit at Parliament it was rather like knocking out the crew of an air-liner. As long as the automatic pilot is intact it stays on course . . . but for a limited period. And then two things can happen. Either a competent crew member recovers in time to take control – or the plane crashes. For the word crash substitute the word revolution. It could happen. You saw that for yourself not many hours ago. You could have led it briefly – and died in it.' He realized the analogy was unfortunate, but couldn't think of a better one. 'The Group wasn't initially looking for revolution, but while its own leadership is intact it can handle it. Their intention was to make you fly the plane at their command. A smooth flight into their own ideology. It didn't happen – and so?' He took the gun out of his pocket and held it on the palm of his hand. 'And so – this. They still have their leaders and while they still have their leaders they're a force to be reckoned with.'

'There are enough right-minded people out there to kick them to hell and back again.'

'Only under strong leadership. The people shouted for you tonight. They need you. Not for an hour. A day. But for a continuing period. They can have your guidance. But not your physical presence. Not yet. What the hell good do you think you could do on your own without professional back-up?' He hesitated – paused. 'I'm sorry. I should speak with more deference, perhaps. Minister this – Minister that. I acted beyond the call of duty getting you to this place tonight – but I got you here because I happen to believe in you and in what you can do. What you can do – in time. At this present moment there's a strong rage in you. Your wife's death has torn your caution to shreds. You can't think straight. That Westminster crowd swung you from one extreme of mood to another. In your broadcast you said you didn't much care if you died. When you were carried shoulder-high you lost your death wish – or rather, you kept it under a different guise. As from then I believe you thought you could take Jackson on in a personal death struggle. Heroics. Bloody heroics. We've no room for them. And no matter what you might feel at this particular moment you can't do violence because basically you're not a violent person. You're a competent parliamentarian who can do some positive good in the future – if you can accept the gift of the future that I'm trying to ram at you. Leave the killing to the killers. We have them. They're trained. They know now who they're after – and they'll get them. That's their job. Tonight Jackson and Harringford openly declared themselves. They knew the hazards, but they believed in their own security network. They're not as strong as they think. Infiltration can work both ways . . . Am I making sense to you?' He hadn't spoken at such length and with such vigour on any other occasion he could remember.

'You're pushing me into a non-combatant role and I think I'm beginning to see the wisdom of it, but for God's sake I can't just sit around. How will the people out there know that anything is being done?'

'You'll tell them. The Group hasn't the monopoly of the press. Until we close *The Galaxy* they'll get their propaganda out. I suggest you supply the free press with counter propaganda. Then there's radio and television. Not yet. Eventually. It will all come in time. You can be read immediately. You will be heard and seen just as soon as it's possible. We'll pull their leaders in and when we do – they'll talk. After that . . .' He spread his hands wide. 'Well – after that – it's back to whatever it was before – minus the complacency. Next time you lot drive me wild with your bickerings in the House I might just forget to spit.'

He stood up and slid the gun across the table. 'Keep it if it gives you any confidence. The men outside have orders to let you go if you demand to go. You are a Minister of the Crown. A man of authority. You ultimately give the orders.' He hesitated then went on reluctantly. 'You can demand that the Group leaders are brought in to stand trial. It would be a foolish order in the present climate, but it would still be obeyed. Or you can demand summary execution on the spot – which will probably happen anyway whether we plan it or not. What would you have us do?'

David picked up the gun. He had never handled one before. It felt alien and cold. He had a momentary vision of Jackson seated across the table from him. He heard Dee's voice on the tape. The screams were less terrible now with the passing of time, but they were terrible enough to make all the nerves in his body flash with pain. He would place the gun in the centre of Jackson's forehead. It would lie against his flesh and he would pull the trigger slowly giving it maximum time.

Or would he?

Would he at the last minute withdraw? Held back by his nature from the ultimate act.

He didn't know.

The death sentence had been passed by circumstances sometime back. Foster had said that the command was his. Let someone else pull the trigger, but let it be done.

'A trial,' he said, 'even if it were possible, would be an act of lunacy.'

'I agree. So as from now all methods – all decisions requiring immediate action – will be left to me?'

It was, David knew, a pointless question. Foster would do what he believed he had to do without reference to anyone.

'Get them. Anyway you can. But get them. Then do what you must.'

'And in the meantime you're prepared to sit it out here?'

'In the meantime – depending on how long you take.'

Foster wasn't normally an optimist. He believed in stating facts. 'If a chicken loses its head it runs around squawking in a bloody reflex – let's say just that long.' He looked around the austere little room. 'Bearable for a short period. Regard it that way. There's a bathroom down the corridor. I'll send a man up with a dry shirt. The one you're wearing is wet. Anything else you want – ask for.' He glanced at the gun in David's hand. 'That's loaded. You're not used to it. If you have any lingering doubt about the integrity of my men then for Christ's sake ask first and shoot after, I don't want our force depleted any more than it already is. Do you want to keep the gun?'

David hesitated. 'Yes.'

Foster tried a joke. 'Perhaps you'll hand it back to me at the State Opening of Parliament – in case you drop it at the Queen's feet.'

'That will be the day.'

'It will come.'

And so it began to end – quietly – inexorably – with the precision and expertise of a full scale underground military operation. The people went about their business and men died. Passion that had run high at the time of the explosion burst into small conflagrations of violence, but the flames in time burnt low. There was little trust, but there was enough and it would grow. Subtly angled publicity reassured and calmed.

David's room – a prison of loneliness – was a healing place, too. He needed solitude. He needed time to think and he had it in abundance. He recreated Dee in his mind. He saw her. He felt her. He agonized over her – as he had to – before he could let her go.

Foster called frequently and reported what had to be reported. In running the Admiral to ground he had lost several of his own men. The Group's security cordon had been tough opposition. The exercise hadn't sweetened his attitude towards Jackson during the three days he held him for interrogation. He hadn't been easy to break.

'The Admiral,' he told David briefly, 'was reluctant to impart some necessary information. Only the senior members of the Nucleus knew the identity of the man at the top – the Leader – the kingpin. We had to know, too.'

David who was fiddling with some chess pieces on a board that he had sent out for picked up one of the pieces and let it drop.

'But surely Harringford . . .?'

'He was to be the strong arm of the triumvirate – you, had you agreed, were cast for the role of political persuader – but the brain behind the set-up was the man Mackilroy took your wife to the night before they died. Owner farmer. Several thousand acres. Paranoid belief in the sanctity of the Mason land – equally paranoid belief that it would be wrested from him. Mackilroy obviously didn't know, which speaks a lot for the security – until now – of the Group. They were friends – or had been.' The diabolical irony of it had struck him as funny at the time, but looking at David now any last vestige of humour went. 'I'm sorry.'

David began placing the chessmen on the board. His fingers were leaden and his breathing harsh. He felt very cold. He had believed Jackson solely responsible for Dee's death. He broke a long silence. 'Go on – you have more to say – say it.'

'We didn't know about Mason and we let him slip. Perhaps under the circumstances it was just as well.'

David looked at him sharply. 'I don't understand you.'

'He and his wife were found in their car in a country lane near the farm this morning. They had died of carbon monoxide poisoning. I have the suicide note. It's long. It's wordy. It's sick. It's the Group's requiem. When you read it I think you'll believe as I do that it should be published. Absolutely as it is. Un-edited. It's the strongest piece of ammunition we could hope for.' He took the long manilla envelope out of his brief-case and put it on the table.

David said, 'Later. I'll read it later.' He needed clarity of thought – a quietness of mind – to be able to assess it. He couldn't bring himself to touch it now with hatred blurring his senses. 'Tell me about Jackson.'

'He's dead.' It was abrupt.

'As a result of the interrogation?'

'There was no physical brutality.'

It was an evasion. David didn't press the point.

'And Harringford?'

'We couldn't risk putting him on trial . . . Well, you've seen him . . . medals and all.'

'And so?'

Foster shrugged. 'He was caught in cross-fire when some of his own men opened up. And if you think that's a convenient, conscience absolving retreat from the truth – then think it. There's been a lot of blood on both sides. I haven't burdened you with a description of the way my men have died. But they have died – believe me – and bloodily.'

By the end of the following week Foster decided that the security precautions could be slackened. 'There's no real need for you to stay here any longer,' he told David. 'The threat is minimal. You'll have a bodyguard as long as you need one. Your fellow MPs are chafing at the bit. It seems time you gathered them around you in a holy alliance and formed a new government.'

David saw the look in his eyes and replied with a reluctant smile. 'Thanks.'

'For doing my job? Think nothing of it.'

'For making it easier to do mine.' For dimming the screen in my mind so that I see without seeing too clearly – but clearly enough to be able to go on. He didn't voice it.

He hadn't liked Foster's methods and Foster had known he hadn't liked them, but they had brought results. The nation was becoming stable again. As from now he would have to start building on the foundation that Foster and his men had swept clean for him. The time of waiting was over.

Foster asked him what his immediate plans were. 'You'll need somewhere to live. I suppose it will have to be an hotel – unless you'd like to put up for a while in my place in Sloane Square. Nothing has been done to your flat.'

'What about the Belvedere – is it still functioning?'

'The nursing home? Yes, it's still functioning – but with a depleted staff. That thump you had on your head isn't still paining you, is it?'

'No. There's someone I have to see.'

Foster dredged up the information that had lain docketed at the back of his mind as not of immediate importance, but pending. 'She's still there. She's getting better. She's a Group member and she planted a bomb. She hasn't been arrested. Yet.'

He eyed David closely. 'It would be quite unethical for you to interfere with the course of justice.'

'Justice? Have we been concerned about justice? Summary executions – is that justice?'

'You agreed to it earlier – verbally.'

'And if I insist now on another sort of justice – verbally?'

Foster gave a short amused laugh. 'It seems to me you're going to do a lot of insisting. Well, good luck to the best of it. It might just work. The other had to.'

* * *

It was evening when David went into Briony's room. She was lying on her side asleep. The scars on her face were like blue hieroglyphics. He had forgotten how badly the bomb had ripped her. But the scars would fade and she could see. A little. Enough to make life bearable. He put his hand on hers in the old gesture of reassurance and stroked her fingers gently.

Bearable.

In time everything had to be better than bearable.

He tried to see the future and realized that he was beginning to see it with more confidence. Power was being thrust on him, but at least he didn't have to wield it alone. It was too early yet to be able to assess the strength and weakness of the new Government. It was embryonic, but with a lusty will to live. The people would nurse it along for a while. They wanted it, and that was the main thing. The brickbats would come later and when they did everyone could relax. All would be normal.

He was aware that Briony was waking slowly. She turned her head to him and then lay as still as a cat. 'David.'

Not a question. She could see him.

'Yes.'

The smile began in her wounded eyes before it reached her mouth. He began smiling, too, naturally and spontaneously and warmly and with the first touch of happiness he had known for a long time.